CHAOS

Sherry Michelle

ISBN:0615459382
ISBN-13: 978-0615459387

Library of Congress Number: 2010915908

Model on the cover: Elicia Jones

Photo taken by: Maximum Xposure Photography

DEDICATION

Thank you to my readers:

As my first novel, it has been a long journey from beginning to end with the creation and completion of Chaos. A manuscript derived from pure imagination and lots of free time. If anyone would have told me five years ago that I was going to write a novel, I would've never believed them. What started off as a hobby, quickly turned into a strong passion for me, and I strive to continue writing great stories that stimulate my reader's imagination, as well as provide those of us who live outside of the box with great alternative reading material. I truly hope you enjoy reading Chaos and thanks to all for your continued support.

Remember a dream will always remain a dream, unless you induce life into it. ~ Sherry Michelle

ACKNOWLEDGMENTS

First and foremost, thank you to my Father above for blessing me with the talent of creative writing, and the fearlessness of constructive criticism.

A special thank you to my partner La Shonda, I love you dearly. It's because of your constant dedication and encouragement that I was motivated to complete Chaos. Not to mention, how selflessly you gave of your time; proofreading pages after pages for me. I know it was redundant, but you hung in there and for that I'm truly grateful. To my kids, who gave unselfishly of their quality time with me, especially during the final days of Chaos, thank you, and I love you both for that. Without your understanding and support, I would not have had a clear conscious, enabling me to focus on my dream. To my mother, although you are not allowed to read any of my books (smile), thank you for constantly believing in me and supporting all my endeavors, I love you. And lastly, but not least, a big thank you to all those who read my manuscript during its embryo stage and for the rave reviews which aided in the finalization of Chaos.

Chapter One

Damn! Another wasted night and my best performance yet. Had I been fucking myself, I would've bust a nut too. Hell, in this case maybe I should've been. I truly wonder if I'll ever experience a mind-blowing, earth-shattering orgasm like the ones we all read about in those kinky love novels. But until that day finally comes, I'll just continue to please myself and mislead my boyfriend Malik into thinking he's laying it down in the bedroom (not).

Poor Malik, all that humping and bumping; winding and grinding; hooting and hollering, and for what? Damn, I should've had a V8 instead.

Look at him, lying here smothering me in all his perspiration. Ugh, I am so over him.

The time had come for him to leave. I had some seriously unfinished business to take care of between my thighs, and his presence was neither needed nor desired any further. Shit, my kitty was purring and was in desperate need of some long overdue TLC.

Irritated by his uselessness, I insisted, "Malik, time to get up. It's getting late. It's the weekend and your office closed several hours ago. Now, get your ass up!" Smiling, but truthfully speaking, "Don't be confused by thinking you gonna move in here with me once your wife kicks your butt out for infidelity."

I nudged him out of his relaxed state of being, as he slowly stood to his feet. "Stop fronting, Danielle. You know you would love to have big poppa here everyday at your every beck and call." Malik lazily reached down and scratched his balls the way men so crassly did and sauntered, sashayed towards the shower with a look of accomplishment etched upon his face.

What a damn shame, I thought shaking my head as I sat and watched Malik walk into the bathroom. *All that man…what a tragic waste.* Disgusted, I waited impatiently for him to do whatever it was he needed to do so he could go home and pretend to be a monogamous loving husband. It didn't bother me that he was about to go lay with another woman. What got my panties in a knot (had I still had on some) was that I was the mistress, yet my pussy walls were just as dry as they were before we started. Silly me, I thought the mistress was supposed to get the "good dick." I guess Malik didn't get that memo.

Sex between us probably wouldn't have been so disappointing had he taken the time to explore my desires just a little. A simple tease, even a kiss south of my belly button from time to time might have actually triggered a real climax during sex. Unfortunately for me, Malik wasn't always an active or willing participant when it came to putting his mouth on or near anything that bled once a month. So, instead, once again I was alone.

The shower came on and as he wiped away all evidence of our lovemaking, or lack thereof, I couldn't help but think about his wife Angela. Don't get me wrong; I didn't give a damn about her. I was sleeping with her husband after all. It just amazed me how none-the-wiser she remained about my year-long affair with her husband. For a black woman, she was pretty damn square. Most black women I knew would have clocked there husband's whereabouts hour by hour; especially with all the late night and weekend work, but not her. Malik and I had gone away together many weekends and there had not been so much as a late night phone call from dear sweet Angela. With a wife like her, fucking around behind her back was a piece of cake.

It didn't take much. Malik would convincingly tell her that the trip was a "company-sponsored" event and I was his personal assistant (yeah real personal) working closely with him and his clients. Because Angela believed in her man and her marriage, she never once suspected her loyal husband of eight years of cheating. She was so uninvolved in his social and work life that I had been able to call their house whenever he was running late for one of our dates. Yes, I know, that was both bold and grimy, but I was checking for my man. Shit, somebody had to put a leash on his ass because she definitely didn't have one on him.

Not only did she not question who I was, but volunteered information on her husband's whereabouts whenever I called. Can you believe that shit? I don't know about you, but any woman calling my house asking for my man better have some type of blood relation-either his mother, his sister, his cousin, or even his aunt. Otherwise, the only thing she would gain from that phone call was a crucial ass cursing out.

I can't figure out for the life of me why Malik married her. They were the complete opposite of one another. He was spontaneous, a thrill seeker, laid back, and he loved his women feisty, much like me. Angela on the other hand was the exact opposite. She was very timid and reserved, at least that's the picture he painted for me. She wouldn't know how to relax unless it was scheduled in on her daily planner. It was no wonder he was sexually bored at home. From what he told me, I completely understood why Malik came looking for me; he needed an outlet from his stale reality. Malik longed for excitement and spontaneity, but overall he desired a more sexually aggressive woman, the type of woman who didn't have to schedule in "sex" on her to-do-list as though it were a daily chore.

"Pass me a towel," Malik yelled as the shower came to a halt. Grabbing a white full-body length towel from my linen closet, I watched as steam escaped through the crack of the bathroom door as I pushed it open. That was the most steam I'd seen resulting from an act of Malik's in the past four months. Holding my composure the best I could, I admired his stature as he flexed his muscles in the steamy bathroom mirror. He prided himself like that of a man who had just laid down some real serious pipe in the bedroom. I had to laugh as I shook my head and allowed him to play out his self-proclaimed victory over my pussy. I must admit, it was quite amusing watching him admire himself in that manner. Apparently, he had no clue that our bedroom habits were in danger of becoming extinct by the way he carried on in that mirror.

Although the sex between the two of us had been a little whack lately, I must give props where props were due. Standing at 6'3" with dark milk chocolate flowing from head to toe, the brother was fine as fuck. Malik was an aficionado when it came to working out and being fit, so naturally everything about him starting from his neck to his chest, downward to his arms, thighs, and legs, even his ass all protruded with masculinity. Yes ma'am, he was all man. Any woman could see that.

Carefully, I observed him as he stood naked before me, and somehow my current dissatisfaction seemed obsolete. Instead, the reasons I fell for him in the first place were rekindled for that brief moment. Chills went through my body as I revisited those first butterflies and for a moment, I felt the way I should've felt earlier during our lovemaking. I was appreciative of my current disposition and entertained those feelings for the remainder of his stay.

Things between Malik and I had not always been this way. Once upon a time, we were one of the hottest couples Miami had ever seen. Our sexual chemistry was nothing short of volcanic, and our fiery presence was felt each and every time we entered a room. We exemplified an electrifying and powerful couple (on the surface) both in the bedroom and out in the streets.

My feelings of sexual deprivation didn't begin until after we consummated a ménage a trois a little while back. That experience was unparalleled to any other experience I'd ever had. It was so intense, that Malik always remained clueless as to how I truly felt about that night. We had played around with the idea of inviting someone new to our bed. We agreed that once it was over and we had our fun that we would never speak on it again. It was to forever remain hidden deep within the confines of all the other deceitful relationship secrets we had acquired over the course of our involvement.

Malik would never admit to it, but I knew I wasn't the only one changed from that one night. A prideful man such as he was would rather die before admitting that another woman threatened his manhood. One would've thought that I suggested the whole thing by how paranoid he acted thereafter, but honestly the idea was solely his.

Never in a million years had I fathomed the thought of being with another woman, not until he propositioned me with it. So like most women, I wanted to please my man by any means necessary—even if it meant going outside of my own comfort zone. As a result, I appeased to his desires and agreed to go through with it against my better judgment. Regrettably, on his behalf, Pandora's Box was officially and irrevocably opened.

<u>*Chapter Two*</u>

I hadn't known exactly what steps to take to solidify Malik's plan of having a ménage a trois, so he suggested I start by going online to a website called *Blackplanet*, an Internet networking and dating site. Each person was asked to register by creating a username for his or her customized page.

There were options available for easy personalization of *Blackplanet's* page including uniquely designed backgrounds, picture uploads, and a large variety of wallpapers and themes. Of course, I opted not to put my photos online because I needed my identity to remain anonymous. I was a professional within my Fortune 500 Corporation, and couldn't run the risk of ever being exploited should my profile fall into the wrong hands. I had to be careful. Besides there were way too many creepy perverts occupying the web nowadays. One could never be too careful.

The cool thing about *Blackplanet* was that it provided people the opportunity to attract specific types of people through their online profile. To my surprise, half of the people on the website were gay, lesbian, transgender or bisexual. Wow, was my initial thought once I started perusing the numerous members' profiles. Malik specifically told me to make my page appealing to bisexual and/or lesbian women only. He wanted to make sure the message being relayed on my page was clear of any inclinations that I was looking for a male companion and I selflessly obliged his request.

My chosen online name was "Bi-curiously kinky." I figured it would attract more bisexual women versus the "hard-core" aggressive butch lesbians. I wasn't looking for a continuous relationship and I'd heard that "real" lesbians, the ones that have never been with a man before didn't care much for bisexual women anyway. They called bisexuals "dick dykes" whatever that meant.

Anyway, my page layout had an eccentric, but erotic theme. I wanted my profile page to stand out among the rest by being creative. My chosen colors for the backdrop were black for mystery and royal blue for a calm soothing contrast. I placed illuminating silhouettes of flickering candles accompanied by the smooth sounds of soft jazz within the layout. This helped to lure my viewers in. As a final touch to my profile I created a scrolling banner that read: *Ladies Only!* I put that in place as a road map for my lost brothers who didn't quite get the hint while reading my user name.

After I was done creating my cyber world on *Blackplanet*, I nervously began to send out friend requests and hello messages to unsuspecting users of the site. I didn't know what type of responses or people I would inevitably encounter, but I was flattered and relieved when I received my first friend request from Ariel Langley. Her approach was genuine and very much welcomed. We connected from our very first conversation, which lasted for several hours.

Late one night I got online for a quick moment just to see had she written me since I accepted her friend request. Luckily for me, she was online checking her messages and noticed that I was logged in; she sent me an IM. "Hello Bi-curiously kinky," she wrote. I was so nervous; I didn't know what to say to her.

"Hello," I replied. My stomach was tied up in all kinds of knots as I awaited her response.

Then finally after a few minutes had passed she wrote back, "You're up late young lady. Don't you think you should be getting your beauty rest?"

She made me smile. I was ecstatic that she didn't come at me like some old pervert up late at night. Unfortunately, most people believed that if you were up late and on the Internet you had to be up to no good, but not Ariel. The time of day didn't matter to her. She talked with me as if it was the top of the morning and the sun was shinning high up in the sky. During that first conversation we talked until the break of dawn.

As the days passed, Ariel and I kept in touch making sure to talk on a daily basis. The chemistry between the two of us was a perfect blend of curiosity and excitement. Once I got over the fact that she was a woman I was pursuing for the sole purpose of sexual gratification, I was able to freely open up to her. Actually, she managed to reverse my intentions and I became the pursued instead of the pursuer. I didn't mind. I quite enjoyed it. At first I thought it was sweet and funny, but soon I grew dependent on receiving her good morning texts and "thinking about you" emails throughout the day. It was too cute, like having a high school crush except we were friends as well. We chit chatted about everything just like real girlfriends often did. With such an authentic connection between the two of us it was as if we had known each other for years. So undeniably I took to her, and she to me.

Throughout our numerous chats, we explored all there was to know about each other, from our likes to our dislikes, as well as our most self-proclaimed successes and failures. I would talk to her in detail about my relationship with Malik and she talked about her last girlfriend. Listening to her go on so vehemently about her relationship with another woman was very strange to hear, but at the same time very intriguing. Two women in a committed relationship; I couldn't wrap my mind around it. Really, what did two coochies do together? After you both go down on each other, then what? Of course, I didn't say any of that to Ariel because I didn't want to insult or demean her sexual preference. But personally, myself, I needed a thick stiff rod right after a good head job.

Surprisingly, Ariel had been in a committed relationship with a man five years prior to meeting her ex girlfriend. She and her ex boyfriend at the time had been together for six years before finally splitting up. When I asked her the infamous question we all ask lesbians: "What made you decide to be with women?" She told me that it was not her decision to make; it was the way she was born. She admitted to me that she had known of her attraction to the same sex since her adolescent years, but she was always too ashamed to act on them. This forced her to remain hidden in the closet for most of her life because like most closeted homosexuals, she too, was afraid of unmasking her true identity in public due to the harsh, unwelcoming way society treat gay people.

But after years of trying without satisfaction to hide, she made a life choice to stop living a lie by denying who she was meant to be on the inside. Because she had had a good and communicative relationship with her former boy friend she had been able to sit down with him one evening for an unveiling of her immaculately concealed sexuality. Although they both cared deeply for one another, and had planned to become engaged, they agreed to part as friends. With no regrets on either part, they still remained the best of friends who loved each other very much.

Unlike Malik and I, there were no secrets between me and Ariel. She had been completely open with me from day one and I appreciated that about her. She shared her life experiences with me about being out and forewarned me that the grass wasn't always greener on the other side.

Amongst her revelations, there were some beautiful stories about how she felt the first time she kissed a woman, along with intoxicating reminisces about the first time she made love to a woman, and the extreme intensity that surrounded her once she fell in love with a woman for the first time. But she also spoke on some real sad stories that broke my heart. They weren't too different from the ups and downs of any normal relationship gay or straight, but unfortunate all the same.

One night, while on the phone, Ariel and I had a confessional. She openly admitted to me that she liked the fact that I was a virgin in the lesbian game. And that it was a strong turn on for her and somewhat of a fantasy come true. Ariel had always wanted to be someone's first and now she would get her chance thanks to me. The whole idea seemed really odd at first. Call me green, but I thought you could only have one first, and that was the first guy who popped your cherry. Don't think of me as a whore, but my cherry had been popped for quite some time. So when she told me she wanted to be my first it threw me for a loop. I guess gay people had their own set of rules for their lifestyle.

As we talked I learned more about the type of women Ariel was attracted to. She preferred her woman to be light skinned with straight pearly white teeth; long natural hair with a slim waistline accentuating the curve of her ass. Cute in the face and not too bulky in the chest area, a C cup to be exact; fortunately for me I was damn near a perfect match. My hair was shoulder length a little shorter than she liked and I was blessed with D cups instead of Cs, but close enough. Everything else was right on point. I was fairly light skinned and at 5'5" I was a little on the short side, but she had no height preference. I was definitely small in the waist with a rotund ass, and I always received ample compliments about how white and bright my smile was. Not to toot my own horn, but I was extremely easy on the eyes. Shit, Malik wasn't risking his marriage over chopped liver.

After several weeks of steady conversation with Ariel, Malik had grown quite impatient and insisted on meeting her. I didn't think we were ready for that just yet, but he didn't care about what I thought as usual. He was adamant about moving forward, but I was persistent about waiting a little while longer. So against his wishes, I decided to keep Ariel to myself longer than the agreed amount of time, which happened to only be one month. I didn't feel that I could properly get to know her or anyone well enough in such a short period of time. This was going to be the first time I crossed over and I wasn't taking it lightly. I wanted to really know her for more than just the obvious purpose. Incapable of having control over my feelings any longer, the more I socialized with Ariel, the stronger my attraction to her became.

I was unable to stall Malik any further so, we all decided to meet on a Saturday night, exactly two months following the first time Ariel and I had officially spoken. In an effort to remain concentrated on the purpose of our engagement, we spoke often about Malik and his likes and mannerisms pertaining to the bedroom. Honestly, the thought of sharing her with him started to disturb me. I no longer wanted Malik to be apart of this planned event, but I knew that would never happen, not in this lifetime. Every fiber of my being desperately wanted our one night together to mean more then just a one-night stand or merely a curious fuck.

The venue had been selected, a very public non-private place. South Beach was infamous for its influx of patrons to the variety of nightclubs and we figured it would be better to meet somewhere safe and not too intimate. There was no place more public and non-private than the nightclubs scattered along the streets of South Beach. Since we were all familiar with *Club Deep* located on the street behind the busy strip, it became our designated meeting point.

A few nights prior to our meeting, Ariel had conveyed to me that she was not the slightest bit interested in Malik anymore, actually she never had been. In fact, she wanted me all to herself, but understood the agreement we had already made weeks ago. Her feelings for me had blossomed ten-fold and she was willing to do whatever it took to make me happy. Truth of the matter, my feelings were mutual towards her. I wanted nothing more than to sneak away with her and go somewhere less crowded and more intimate, somewhere that was suitable for a first date, and forget all about Malik and his twisted wants of a ménage a trois.

The more Ariel dissected the ins and outs of being in a lesbian relationship the more intrigued I became with the whole woman-on-woman thing. Never would I have guessed that women had so much game. Men often spoke on how manipulative we women were, but I never understood what they meant until I experienced it first hand myself. Ariel may not have been aware that she was spitting mad game, but whatever she was or wasn't doing had a fixed hold over me.

She was different and she kept my mind racing as I held on to every word that came out of her mouth. She was sincere in all she said; I never doubted anything she ever told me. Whenever we spoke, her attentiveness made me feel like I was all that mattered, and she'd always let me know that I was a constant thought on her mind, with consistent emails and texts throughout the day. It had been such a long time since I was made to feel so desired. It was weird to have been coming from a woman, but I cherished every minute of it.

Club Deep's parking lot was almost at capacity and the streets of South Beach were already buzzing with tourists and night walkers. Malik and I purposely arrived a few minutes early. We wanted to scope Ariel out before she had a chance to see us. I needed this night to be perfect and I wanted to be perfect for her as well. Earlier in the week I did some personal maintenance in preparation for tonight: a facial, a manicure, pedicure, new hairstyle, a new "fuck me" dress with matching pumps, arched eyebrows, and for dessert a Brazilian bikini wax…Ouch! I was never one to be hairy anyway, but Ariel had mentioned that she liked a clean-shaven pussy, so I made sure (no matter how painful) that it was as clean and as smooth as a baby's bottom.

Recalling the description of Ariel's vehicle from a prior text, she finally arrived at the club about ten minutes after Malik and I. Pulling up in a flawless black BMW convertible with the top down and mocha-colored leather interior, I took heed to how perfectly blended the inside of her car matched her smooth tanned complexion. With the light sea breeze coming in from the Atlantic Ocean, it made for a perfect night to take a stroll along the shoreline, which happened to be located right behind the club.

Anxiously we watched as Ariel climbed out of her car, long legs first. She was a curvaceous beautiful black woman, about 5'6" with a hypnotic frame. Her flowing hair danced gently against the airy night as she cautiously approached us. I could smell the enchanting scent of ripened roses and tuberose just moments before she stood face-to-face with me and Malik. Beautifully slightly slanted light brown eyes and high prominent cheekbones, this woman was nothing short of a bonafide Nubian Princess.

"Ariel," I presumed extending my hand as a formal gesture.

"Yes, Danielle?" She took my dangling hand. Wow, was the only word that made sense to me at the moment. How could a woman this beautiful be gay, I silently questioned? Her hand was as soft as butter as I held on to it, as if not to ever let go.

Clearing his throat, Malik rudely interrupted, "Aren't you going to introduce me to your friend?" Not really, I was dying to say. Then without any further hesitation, I reluctantly introduced Ariel to Malik.

They too shook hands and his approval was gloriously plastered all over his face. "Don't smile too hard Malik," I teased him half-heartedly. Although I hated to admit it, part of me was a little jealous about his reaction towards her. I mean he was smiling so hard you could literally see all 32 of his damn teeth. Keeping in mind what that night was all about, I forced myself to relax and not get bent all out of shape. This was an indulgence for us all. Besides, I couldn't blame him for how he reacted. Shit my first response towards her was no better. The woman was beautiful there was no doubt about that. She was even more beautiful than I ever imagined her to be. Blatantly smitten by Ariel's physical physique, we were both extremely satisfied and giddy about the remainder of our evening.

Chapter Three

That one official look at Ariel outside in the parking lot left me incomprehensibly hooked. Don't ask me how, especially since I had never looked at another woman like that before. But the mind is a mysterious vessel. I had already taken a genuine liking to her before our meeting so, I knew her physical appearance would have no real bearing towards my feelings for her. Personality-wise she was addictive, but in no way was I prepared for her immeasurable outer beauty. I swear to you; I couldn't take my eyes off of her not even for a minute. It was as though I was under some type of hypnosis and she had complete and utter control over me.

Inside the substantially small club the atmosphere was dark, cold, and damp. There were two fully stocked bars located along the wall on either side of the vacant space. There was plenty of elbow room to maneuver around the club for the moment. Grateful for the cool climate I exhaled a little. This was not the time for Ariel to see me sweat just yet. There would be plenty of time for that later.

Multi-colored strobe lights danced on the ceiling in unison as a fog machine filled the room every ten minutes like clockwork. Hip-hop and R&B thumped loudly from the massive speakers mounted to the walls and in no time we were nodding our heads and two-stepping to the beats as we sipped on the first of many drinks to come. Nearby in a corner VIP space I noticed something white and folded sitting in the middle of one of the table pieces: **Reserved for Malik Michaels**. I wasn't surprised. Malik was a man of status, so reserving a VIP spot even in a small establishment like *Club Deep* was a must for him. He wouldn't be caught dead anywhere without at least having the option to be classified as **V**ery **I**mportant **P**eople.

"This way ladies," he said, pointing us in the direction of the small reserved table. Malik signaled for a waitress to attend to us and sat down on my left while Ariel sat to my right. The vibrant, young waitress waited as Malik arbitrarily ordered a bottle of Veuve Clicqout and three champagne flutes. Why? I don't know. He was being flashy thinking that was what all women wanted, a man who was not afraid to flaunt his finances. That may have been true for some women looking for a quick come up, but both Ariel and I were gainfully employed and financially stable. But I allowed him to show boat, especially since this was a special night for Ariel and me. We had wanted to see each other for a long time now and thanks to Malik we got to do it on his dime.

After the bottle of Veuve Clicquot and a couple glasses of white merlot I was pleasantly intoxicated. The full effects of the mixtures of alcohol within my blood stream summoned my body to the dance floor like a bee to honey, evoked by the lyrics of the song "Yes," from artist Floetry.

Ariel equally liberated by her own feel good blend of alcohol, sensed my sexual energy and finally joined me on the dance floor.

There was no sense of nervousness at all; more like a hunger had taken over my sensual side as I watched Ariel come closer to me. Animalistic thoughts ran through my mind and my blood ran hot as I anticipated her final destination. Suddenly sensitized to touch of any kind, my breathing grew shallow and rapid as Ariel rubbed along the side of my arm in passing.

Already in her own groove, she planted herself directly behind me and began to slow grind to the rhythm of the music. No longer shy, no longer connected by just voice over the phone and intuitive of her rising nature, my heart damn near leaped out of my chest as she slid her hand down my neck passing the arch in my back, and then finally reaching my thighs. With her fingertips, she outlined my curvy figure as we swayed side to side collectively to the amorous sounds of Floetry. For lack of better words it was safe to say that we were both fucking horny!

Turning me to face her, Ariel guided my sweaty hands up in the direction of her breasts. With our fingers intertwined, she joined me in grabbing a handful of her own soft flesh beneath her thin top. I lowered my head slightly and watched as her chest rose and fell through each panting breath. So perfectly rounded and soft to the touch, I desired to feel her breasts in their bare form. I wanted to explore all the senses associated with her; what she looked like, what she smelled like, and how she tasted in her natural essence.

Already to the point of spontaneous combustion, Ariel then unzipped the zipper of my skin-tight, low-rise denim jeans and guided her hand south of the border. Taken by surprise she realized that I wasn't wearing any panties, but that didn't stop her as she continued her journey down south.

Simultaneously, both of our breathing became heavier as she reached the split between my thighs that separated women from men. Wet as hell, she teased me by playing around the entrance of my body. I craved her and I leaned forward to kiss her gently on the neck, while trying my hardest to suppress the rapidly growing orgasm brewing within my mid section. To no avail, involuntary moans still managed to escape through my parted lips as she practically finger fucked my pulsating pussy right there in the midst of all those who surrounded us. Hearing the sounds of acceptance slither off my vocal cords naturally her hand slid deeper into my wetness. "Ooh… you're so fucking wet," she whispered in my ear.

Briefly I broke away from my own indulgence and hinted to Malik to come join us on the dance floor. Judging by the sinister smirk on his face he seemed to be enjoying the performance from where he stood. We really didn't need him. I would've been content with the night ending with just Ariel and I, but that was not the agreed upon arrangement made between Malik and me.

He demonstrated a little more swagger in his stride than he normally did as he slowly and methodically moved toward us, canvassing the crowd as he did. He wanted to make sure all eyes were on him as he walked up to the two most beautiful women in the club. Cautiously, I stepped aside and allowed the two of them to become more familiar with one another.

Malik wrapped his massive arms around Ariel's small waist and pulled her closer into him. The two of them dancing so close and full of lust provoked every sexual nerve in my body. He was being extremely gentle with her, which reminded me of why I fell in love with him in the first place. It was those same traits that I use to admire about him in the beginning of our relationship. In that instant I wished I could have frozen time only long enough to feel what I once felt for him a little while longer.

I was engorged with so many emotions: love for him, lust for her, lust for him, and jealousy of her. Deliberately, I positioned myself between the two of them; forcing us all into a compromising position. Our bodies were pressed firmly against one another on the dance floor. My overwhelming desire to be touched took precedence over all things; I felt the need to be groped by the both of them and preferably at the same time.

Mmm...tuberose; the scent teased my nostrils again. Ariel's fragrance generously bounced off her onto me. I couldn't help but wonder if she tasted as good as she smelled. Unknowingly to her, my freshly shaven pussy was saturated with anticipation and intensely thumping to the point of painful pleasure. I had no clue that a woman was capable of sexually exciting me at all, especially to this degree.

Sinfully, I craved her like a prisoner craved his freedom. It had become crystal clear that the time for us to leave the club scene had come. Things had gotten way too hot and explicitly dangerous for us to still be present in public. Malik took control of the situation and led us from the dance floor, as he simultaneously flagged the waitress to bring our tab. Hand in hand Ariel and I followed intently behind our leader.

Outside the club Miami had really come to life. Streets were lined with flashy overly exaggerated cars and illuminated club marquees lit up the busy platforms of Collins Ave. All types of people walked the streets of South Beach nightly from the typical white-collar corporate American, to the late night pole dancers from the hoods of Liberty City. Whatever your pleasure, South Beach was definitely a perfect place to come to lose one's self, even if only for one night. Luckily for us it was also infamously known for its prominent chain of resort style hotels.

Malik carefully guided us through the hustle and bustle of the active strip; finally we reached the parking lot where both vehicles remained. Malik suggested we take his truck and leave Ariel's car behind. In agreement, she checked her BMW one last time making sure anything of value was tucked neatly away out of clear view. In pure admiration of her, I watched as she bent over searching the back seat and floor for anything that may be enticing to a passing thief or a starving vagrant. Mesmerized by the apple shape of her ass, I silently prayed for a gust of wind to suddenly rush by to cause her dress to slightly take flight and reward me with a sneak preview of what lay beneath. Regrettably, I had no such luck.

Malik unlocked the doors to his materialized mechanical twin, and helped Ariel and I into the back seat of his robust, black, and irresistibly gorgeous Special Edition H2 Hummer. The backseat was big with plenty of maneuvering room and his newly installed stereo system thumped lightly to the sounds of Barry White, Al Green, and Keith Sweat. I noticed the two-dozen yellow roses and a bottle of Moet strategically placed on the tan leather seats for our benefit just moments before we entered the vehicle. Yeah, Mr. Smooth had thought of everything.

Ariel and I nestled close to one another in the carefully constructed ambiance as Malik maneuvered down the cluttered strip toward our hotel. He foolishly swerved in and out of the Saturday night traffic as though the truck was on autopilot while he watched our rousing interaction with one another through the rearview mirror. "Malik you may want to keep your eyes on the road," I cautioned from the back seat as I caressed the sides of Ariel's face. At this point I was absolutely fearless, and I had no regard for what I was doing or for what was being done to me. Alcohol proved once again without a doubt to be a nervous girl's best friend. With all inhibitions aside, one could have easily assumed by my actions that I was not new to this lifestyle.

Focused on me and completely absent-minded of anyone or anything else around her, Ariel gazed into my eyes while stroking the hair that dangled near my face. Slowly she turned toward me and asked, "May I kiss you?" I nodded as she leaned in and gave me one of the softest mind-blowing kisses I had ever had. I believe her asking my permission was a way to make sure I was coherent, comfortable, and accepting of what was happening. I thought that was a sweet and commendable gesture. No one had ever asked permission before kissing me before; I guess that was just one of the many differences between being courted by a woman versus a man; a formality I really appreciated.

After a short, yet intense ride, we managed to reach our destination. Malik stepped out of the truck and handed the keys to valet. Malik redeemed our reservations at the front desk of the Ritz-Carlton, located right off the main strip of Collins Ave. The architectural structure of the building was amazing! The contractors paid extraordinary attention to every minute detail of the extravagant masterpiece. On the ceiling above were elegant sketches of Roman artwork along with massive sparkling chandeliers brilliantly bedazzling guest as they entered the five-star, resort-style hotel. Impressed, I made a mental note to myself to return in the very near future. "This is nice Malik," Ariel complimented his taste.

"Thank you," Malik replied as he retrieved the key to our room. "I wanted to take you ladies somewhere special tonight. Just wait until you two see the suite; it's to die for."

Chapter Four

Staggering out of the elevator onto the 25th floor, we reached the door that would lead us to paradise. Malik inserted the key card and oh my gosh…the room! He was absolutely correct. The two-bedroom suite was undeniably breath taking. The floor plan was huge, at least 1200 square feet with large bay windows overlooking the ocean. I walked to one of the windows and pulled back the curtains slightly to allow the light from the moon to shine through, but only enough to perfect the already perfect setting.

Looking out, I admired the stark contrast of the steel and glass skyscrapers against the backdrop of the tranquil Atlantic Ocean. Miami Beach was spectacular, a carefully crafted paradise playland. I allowed myself to be lost in the gorgeous view for just a moment before concentrating on the view within my suite.

Centered in the living area on top of the cream colored Persian rug were a large black leather sofa sectional and a bottle of chilled champagne in a bucket of ice on one of the end tables. That was exactly what we didn't need … more liquor.

The suite came fully equipped with a full size kitchen, decorative dining area, a big screen plasma TV mounted onto the living room wall, a fireplace - yeah in Florida, and a nice surround sound stereo system. It had everything you could possible need. Exactly what I would expect my honeymoon suite to look like should I ever marry, I thought to myself. But that would require someone proposing to me; something I was clearly not in the running for with Malik. *Reality check.*

Inside the master bathroom, the walls were lined with oversized travertine and the full moon shined through the oval window reflecting off the polished marble tiled floor. Confined behind French style frosted glass doors were three walls and a ceiling of water tiles. I could only imagine the feeling of being drenched in pure jetted pleasure.

Pleased with the décor of the master bath, I grew even more excited at the sight of the deep Jacuzzi tub centered in middle of the room. With my eyes closed, I imagined that Malik and Ariel were busy at play while bubbles fell to the floor creating a white fluffy blanket around them. Smiling to myself, I stepped down into the tub to join my lovers. No longer focused on Malik, Ariel rose from beneath the waters. Her almost exposed breasts were covered only by slow descending bubbles. I knew she wanted me to come to her, but I ignored her silent request and positioned myself in front of the jet stream that hummed near my vagina. Instantly my thighs parted and I felt the pressure from the stream hit my clit just right. I threw my head back and began to move my hips in a circular motion. Ariel soon joined me. She placed herself behind me and wrapped her long legs around my waist. Her fingers massaged my clit as she moved with me against my rhythm. Her pussy was warm and swollen as she slide effortlessly against my skin. Then without notice, I gasped as she inserted two fingers inside my hole causing my pelvic muscles to contract. Ooh….I moaned.

My train of thought was abruptly interrupted by the sound of a cork popping. I glanced across the room and my eyes were met by Ariel's. She smiled while motioning for me to join her and Malik for a drink. I obliged her request. With her arms wrapped around my waist we toasted to the night's events. Then with an innocent kiss to the cheek she sent an intense chill up my spine, as I stood frozen within her embrace.

Witnessing our kiss live and in person, Malik hurriedly topped off our bubbly. "Here you go ladies," he handed us glasses filled to the rim. Quickly, we all sipped to avoid spillage. The chill of the champagne cooled what was burning inside of me for Ariel. I was so ready for this. I needed this…and I wanted her!

After sipping from my glass, I walked to the Jacuzzi to prepare a nice warm bath for us. Ariel stared at me from the bedside while I ran our bath water. "I can't wait to taste you," she mouthed just as Malik walked into the room and sat next to her.

The bulky post style bed sat high up off the floor, layered with an expensive white plush down comforter halfway peeled back as if awaiting our arrival. There was a plethora of neutral colored accompanying pillows adorning the overly emphasized wood-framed headboard. Surveying the suite once more, jokingly I said while nudging Malik, "Damn, why can't I get this kind of treatment on a solo tip with you?"

Smiling he just hugged me saying, "Don't worry baby, you're my queen everyday not just tonight." Sealed with a kiss, he managed to do what he has always been capable of doing; he made me feel like an elementary school girl with her very first crush.

With the smooth melodic sounds of slow jams projecting from the radio, I stood ready to be engulfed by my two lovers. Near the over flowing bubble bath with my slight alcoholic buzz in full throttle, I began to disrobe first unbuttoning my blouse then my pants. As I kept eye contact with Ariel, I single handedly unsnapped my bra and purposely poured champagne down my exposed breast. I teased both of them as I asked, "Who wants some?"

Without hesitation or resistance, Ariel was the first to joyously come and sip from my fully erect nipples. "Ooh…" I moaned as she took my entire D cups into her warm moist mouth. Wrapping her lips around my hardened sensitive nipples, she pulled and sucked pleasantly torturing them and I loved it!

Through my periphery I noticed that Malik had begun to undress himself as well. Watching us enjoy each other turned him on; he began to stroke his hardened cock up and down through his boxer briefs. Out of pure appreciation of his protruding manhood, my pussy began to throb in anticipation of the inevitable. I loved the prodigious size of his dick; the fact that he knew what to do with it was always a bonus.

Controlled by her desires, Ariel was oblivious to her surroundings. Busy working her jaw muscles as she sucked, licked, and gently bit on both my succulent breasts. This drove me crazy, it was as though she knew my body and knew exactly what I liked.

"Damn, baby girl! I want you," escaped her parted lips as she slowly kissed her way up to the base of my neck, then my mouth. Her tongue skillfully maneuvered up and down my midline sending chills from my head to my toes. With a quickened, talented hand, piece-by-piece our clothing hit the floor. I was unsure as to how she managed to undress both of us at the same time, but I wasn't necessarily in the business of asking questions at that moment.

Her skin was velvet textured, hairless, and smooth to the touch, just the way I would've imagined a woman should feel and exactly what I would've expected my woman to feel like had I been one-hundred percent gay. Staring at her in the nude like that was very pleasing and teasing to my tingling erogenous zone. She took a seat on the edge of the Jacuzzi and spread her lengthy legs wide to reveal her hidden pearl to me. "Yes," I could hear Malik over my shoulder rooting her on. The gushing sounds of him stroking his dick grew more rapidly as she sat sprawled open for all to see.

Licking her index and middle fingers, she made sure they were extremely saturated as she massaged and pulled at her sexually aroused clit. For that quick instant, I became envious of her fingers. I wanted it to be my tongue that teased and taunted her engorged clitoris. My pussy began to leak with my own wetness as I seriously yearned to feel her. No, fuck feeling her…I wanted to taste her!

No longer the star of his own one man show, Malik walked up and took Ariel from behind, grabbed her by the waist and slowly kissed down the back of her neck. "Mmm…" she moaned, as she insinuated for me to come closer. As I approached her she began to lick her lips, while Malik worked his way down until he reached her ass. Opening her legs wider, he buried his head underneath in between her legs, ferociously thrusting his fingers deep inside her pussy. "Ah fuck!" she panted upon insertion.

"Damn, your pussy so fucking wet!" he exclaimed while tasting the residual of her premature climax. I had to agree; she was soaked. I could see how saturated she was from where I stood.

Completely emerged in ecstasy, she moaned with pleasure while riding his face and finger fucking my pussy. "That feels good…oh so good!" I said grabbing Ariel by the head wanting her to taste me. Moving her fingers in and out of my already pulsating pussy, she pleasured me as best she could—considering her current position on top of Malik's face. What was this woman doing to me? I had never reached a point of orgasm so quickly with anyone before...Ever!

The essence of sex had already invaded the confines of our space as we made our way to the bed. Malik in all his masculinity stood over me as he dangled his well-endowed 10-inch dick above my head. Salivating, I anticipated taking him whole. My slurping was music to my ears as his dick went in and out of my slippery wet mouth, deep and slow.

"Ooh," he moaned with his head tilted back and eyes closed.

The once earlier scent of tuberose had evaporated from Ariel's body; she was now laced with the sexual fragrance of a woman who had gradually reached her sexual peak. As I serviced Malik, Ariel kissed and massaged my breast making me feel like a woman should. Aroused beyond my wildest dreams, I enjoyed being touched and enticed as I pleasured Malik. *This awesome feel-good feeling could easily become my most sought out obsession,* I thought in between sucking and stroking Malik's fully matured cock.

Hard at work, Ariel worked diligently between my sweaty thighs, kissing all around the outer parts of my jumping cunt; she was driving me utterly insane. It had been awhile since I had any southern loving, so her teasing was getting the better of me. My pussy ached oh so good, as she lightly brushed over it with her moist thick lips. "Ah…" she moaned inhaling my scent. Then without warning, she shoved her tongue deep inside my womanly walls. "Fuck!" I grunted. My mouth full, I almost bit down on Malik's dick.

Below my waistline Ariel's tongue danced gracefully inside of me; she was way too good at what she was doing. Now, I've had my shit eaten before, but never like this. If I hadn't known better, I would've suggested that someone else was down there helping her. *There was no way one person was capable of multitasking this effortlessly,* I thought to myself. Naturally in sync with my body, her attention to detail was impeccable as she fondled my clit with every part of her mouth.

Malik switched positions and took Ariel doggy style as she continued to feast on me. "You like watching her eat my pussy?" I asked him, as I bit my bottom lip.

"Fuck yeah baby, and she looks good eating you too." The visual of his statement must've magnified his level of horniness, because he started pounding the shit out of Ariel. Sincerely concerned for her well being, I checked her facial expression to make sure she was OK with the sudden change in his pace. Through clinched teeth she begged him for more, so I assumed she was OK.

Anxiety from having watched them two in action finally got the better of me, and I insisted on switching places with Ariel. Besides, my curiosity lay in between her thighs. I still wanted to know how she tasted. Impatient, I told Ariel to place herself in front of me and open her legs; for my tongue now yearned to fuck her in the same manner that Malik's dick had recently done.

I wanted to experience the feel of her bald pussy against my face while it glided in my mouth. Following my instructions to the tee and without pause, she lay out in front of me, and Malik knelt down beside her just close enough to still be within the reach of her mouth. Without any further delay, I made my way down the center of her body remembering to pay a great deal of homage to both of her succulent breasts. As I got closer to my destination, my heart sped up; the sexual musk that rose up from her pussy caused my juices to immediately descend. "Thump... thump..." was the sound of my heart franticly beating through my vaginal walls.

As my naked breast raked downward against her body, my perky nipples gently stimulated her dripping wet pussy. The tips of my lips caressed the small patch of pubic hair that remained; intently, I teased her the way she had been teasing me all night.

Then without further ado, with my eyes closed and my body eager, I dove right in. *Slippery, yet tasty,* I thought, as I licked and sucked on her clit like an icicle on a hot summer's day. Beneath my grip her body shook and shivered, unable to shake free of me. I sensed the intensity of an orgasm building as her body prepared for an eruption of pure pleasure.

"Yes…yes, just like that baby!" she screamed. With a tenacious grip on my head, she forced my tongue deeper and deeper inside her. She wanted me to fuck her, and I yearned to grant her wish. The thought of exploring her body in the same manner that Malik had, made my toes tingle and started my own orgasm to rise.

Drunken by the gyration of her body and the sensual sounds that escaped her, my grip tightened around her ass and salaciously, I sucked on her clit a little harder. With my own heat boiling over and no other means of releasing, I was forced to dry hump the corner end of the bed as I imagined that I was riding her face instead. It had become evident that Malik no longer existed to either of us. We were both lost in ecstasy; oblivious to the world around us.

Finally, I reached my orgasmic peak and without the help of Malik or a vibrator; that was definitely a first for me. The sensation traveled upward from my feet through the rest of my body causing my breathing to become short and shallow. I was stunned. But what was even more astonishing was that I was about to cum from eating another woman's pussy! *Wow!* I couldn't believe that this was really happening.

The more Ariel moaned the harder I fucked that damn bed. My pussy had gotten so tender and engorged that I pleaded for the earliest sign of any relief. Then suddenly, Ariel's body bucked, her legs clasped around my head, and the most beautiful sound echoed from deep within her diaphragm, "I'm cumming! Yes, baby I'm cumming!" And together we both did.

Breathless and exhausted, she pulled me to eye level so she could look at me. The affection she had for me was apparent all over her face. The look in her eyes satisfied me and confirmed that tonight meant as much to her as it did to me. For us it was more than just a fuck.

Personally, I was done. I'd achieved what I set out to do, but I knew Malik's balls were in critical need of an ejaculation. So, to make things move along a lot quicker, I positioned myself in his favorite position—sunny side up, and allowed nature to take its course.

He was more aggressive and vocal than I remembered him being when it was just the two of us. Guess seeing another woman do to me what he rarely would— eat my pussy— provoked him into having to prove his manliness once and for all. Men were funny that way. Whenever they felt threatened, they would do something macho to show how much tougher they were versus their opponent. Simple creatures if you ask me.

Hours later or what seemed like hours later we were all pretty tired and fell into a blissful sleep. Of course, Malik was in the middle with Ariel and me to either side of him. The next morning had come too quickly, and we awoke thirsty and famished from the prior night's activities. We ordered room service, and after eating had a repeat session of the previous night festivities. Afterwards, we all took full advantage of the opportunity to bathe in style and finally made it into the luxurious Jacuzzi tub.

Ariel's performance with me must have put Malik in a state of worry, because he stayed hella close to me throughout the remainder of our time together. If ever she and I were given a moment to be alone, he would make sure it didn't happen. I thought this was odd behavior considering the intimate night and morning we all just shared together.

Malik seemed frazzled and rushed as he hurried around the room gathering our clothes. *Did he regret opening Pandora's Box? Was he worried about the irreversible change this act would have on our relationship?* Malik grabbed our things and set them in front of the elevator door outside our suite. Ariel and I stood watching him in an awkward silence. I realized at that moment that living out our fantasies may have caused more harm than good.

Distressed, not wanting to depart from one another, the silent drive back to Ariel's car seemed like an eternity. Malik switched gears and tried his best to make small talk, but Ariel and I weren't listening. We were off together somewhere else. Eventually, he grew tired of talking to himself and just turned the radio on.

Back at her car, the once lively nightlife scene had reached an eerie calm, and it was just a regular day on South Beach. Tourists were window shopping sporting their "I Love Florida" t-shirts, and the locals were doing whatever it was locals did on any given day of the week. Unlike Malik's crude ass that just said "thank you" and "goodbye," before quickly getting back into his truck, I gave Ariel a warm embrace and kissed her softly on her lips. Not wanting to let go, I slowly pulled away but not before a single teardrop fell from her eyes and touched the side of my face.

I too, felt the urge to cry but kept my composure. I mean really, how was I going to explain my compassion for her to Malik? He had made it crystal clear that after our one night of sexual freedom, I was never to be with another woman again. But subconsciously, I knew that last night was just the beginning of chaos!

Chapter Five

It had been a week since our rendezvous with Ariel; and oddly enough I couldn't get her out of my head. I had so many mixed emotions and unanswered questions. How are you completely straight one day, then gay the next? *"Was I gay?"* A question I kept asking myself. I mean I loved Malik, but I definitely missed Ariel. Although the sex was awesome, that was not the part of her I missed most. Not having our daily phone conversations and emails left me with an emotional void. I tried to honor my agreement with Malik and told myself repeatedly to just forget about her, but nothing worked. Desperately, I wanted to make it all a figment of my imagination, but I couldn't deny what had happened. The truth was that last week happened and was as real as it gets.

After two weeks of torment, I yielded to my desires and called her. Surprisingly, she was happy to hear from me. "Hey Danielle, I was wondering how long it was going to take you to call me. How have you been sweetie?" Her voice soothed my nervous spirit. "Um-I've been missing you," the words slipped from my lips before I could catch them. Oops, I thought to myself. Oh well. Too late to take it back now. So, I sat back and waited for her reaction to my Freudian slip. A brief silence hung in the air until she said,

"I've missed you too baby." She took my breath away. And just like that it was like old times between the two of us.

Secret dates and late night phone calls were all I had to offer Ariel in the beginning. Although, she sort of knew that our involvement was not supposed to be she never asked any questions; therefore, I never told her any lies. The one and only time she did ask me about Malik I simply told her he was still around. What I failed to mention was that despite the fact that he was married, we considered ourselves a monogamous couple. And he stood firm to his decision of not wanting me intimately involved with another woman; especially her.

Over the next couple of months I attempted to wean myself off of Ariel, but like a moth to a flame I was drawn to her. Things had gotten a little too close for comfort and I was calling and hanging out with her on a regular basis; dodging Malik every chance I got. Stupidly, one night I confused my engagements between the two of them and almost got caught. I was supposed to be having dinner with Malik, but forgot; therefore, I invited Ariel over for a candle lit meal with benefits. Well… Malik arrived first. He was on time for our date and when he saw how nicely I had the whole place decked out with scented burning candles, soft jazz humming from the surround sound, and a nice see through rose-colored negligee he automatically assumed it was all for him. And since mama ain't raise no fool, I pretended it was all for him as well.

Excusing myself to the bedroom for a quick minute, my fingers trembled; I couldn't dial Ariel's phone number fast enough. "Hello," I said breathless from my heart beating 200 miles a minute.

"Hey you, I'm about five minutes away and guess what I'm wearing?" She sang from the other end of the receiver.

Absentmindedly, I inquired, "What?"

"My birthday suit and a fresh bikini wax just for you. I can't wait for you to see it." Knowing how crazy I was about a hairless twat, I wanted Malik to take his ass home.

Painfully denying myself, "Baby that's awfully tempting, but I regret to tell you that I have to take a rain check tonight. I just got called into an emergency staff meeting and I'm on my way out right now," I lied.

"At this time of night," she questioned?

"Yeah, things like this happen sometimes. It sucks, but that's the price I pay for being the head bitch in charge," I joked trying to lighten her disappointment.

With a heartfelt sigh she responded, "It's OK, honey…really. I understand and respect your work. I hope to hear from you after your meeting." Hanging up with her and with a heavy conscience, I returned to my inopportune dinner with Malik.

Dining with him was different that night. As I watched him feast on my lover's meal, my stomach turned sour and I barely ate. Images of her naked body continuously occupied my thoughts, making me resent Malik's presence even more. Irritable, my kitty throbbed and called for Ariel in the worst way. Squirming around in my seat trying to alleviate some of the pressure, I pressed my pussy hard against the stiff cushion wishing it were Ariel's pussy that pushed back. Not quite the feeling I was looking for, but it was a cheap thrill that sufficed for that moment.

Highly aroused and the total opposite of what I truly desired, I took my frustrations out on the closest person to me. No romance, no foreplay, I didn't want any of that. Just wanting to relieve my agony, I led Malik to the bedroom and literally tore off his clothes. Hell, I could afford to buy him another set if need be.

Throwing him onto the bed and insatiably fucking him, I thought of no one but Ariel. I imagined sucking on her steamy sticky pussy, while fingering her in the ass. Oh, how she loved that stimulating combo, I smiled to myself. Visions of this made me throw my pelvis faster and harder against Malik's enormous dick. With buried nails into his skin and repeated images of making love to Ariel, my body tensed as I reached my orgasmic plateau. Unable to control the bark brewing within my abdomen, involuntarily, I let out the most boisterous howl I'd ever heard. Shocked, yet pleased, Malik stared at me with both confusion and admiration.

Exhausted both mentally and physically, I fought back the tears that had built up in the corner of my eyes, as I lay embraced within Malik's biceps. I felt so guilty about what I was doing and the dangerous game I was foolishly playing. It was bad enough that I was sleeping with a married man, but now I was sleeping with a woman behind his back. This was absolute chaos!

The lying had to stop. Keeping a secret this big from Malik was killing me. Although he lied all the time to his wife, I made it my duty to never lie to him. It was time to end my affair with Ariel, before someone got hurt. The more I thought of leaving her, the more I cringed. My feelings for her were getting too deep and growing too rapidly. I wished my love for Malik was strong enough to stop my body from craving her, but nothing could quench my appetite. I was out of control. I had to end it now, abruptly, before it was too late. I guess when you give in to the temptations of the flesh you run the risk of being hurt. Lesson learned.

Thinking back, I never expressed to Malik my true feelings about that night we shared with Ariel. Maybe I should have and all this may have been avoided. But I knew Malik, and I knew he couldn't handle knowing the truth.

One thing was apparent; I hadn't planned on all this confusion from just one night of great sex. If Malik had any idea that a woman made me cum harder than he ever did, his ego would have been severely damaged. I can't explain how one goes from being "strictly dickly" one day to "wanting clitly" over night. All I can say is something besides great sex happened that night; many months ago. Something within me was awakened. Something I never knew existed. My underlying love for women was born that night. *Real Chaos!*

Chapter Six

It was 2:00 A.M. when my phone rang. I thought it was Malik, but when I answered it was my drama-filled best friend, Maxine, with another episode of "As Maxine Turns." I swear with all the drama she kept in her life that chick really needed her own daytime soap opera show. She and I had been friends for over ten years and I loved her as if she was blood related. No matter how eccentric and non-traditional she may have been, she was my ace and the only real friend I had. Since outing myself to her about my sexuality, she felt compelled to call me at all times of the day and night with her extensive lesbian dramatics.

Lesbianism wasn't anything new to her; she'd been out and proud about her love for women damn near her whole life, or at least for as long as I've known her. She was so happy when I told her about my involvement with Ariel. Although it didn't last long between us, she was content knowing that I at least had the ultimate experience.

"Wake up Danielle; I got some real shit to tell you!" Maxine shouted through the phone.

"Max, its 2:00 A.M. can't this wait?"

"Hell no…Now wake your sleepy ass up now!" she screamed.

"Okay bitch…damn I'm up. This shit better be good too." With that being said she began with her story.

"Girl…you know that Spanish chick I been dating for the past six months; the one with a tight ass like Jennifer Lopez?"

"Yeah…she sexy as hell," I recalled.

"Well that trifling ass bitch claimed to be "100% lesbian" right? Not. I went to her house after the club tonight and she acted like she didn't know me. The bitch wouldn't open or come to the damn door. She had the nerve to tell me I should've called before I came.

Now Danielle, you know how I feel about being disrespected. I told that bitch she had three seconds to voluntarily let me in, or I was going to cave her shit in. Cowardly, she asked me to go home and wait for her to call me. Now when she said that I knew something was up. She either had company or someone was on their way over. Keeping in mind that she always left her bedroom window open, I told her OK, I'll leave; but I didn't.

Instead, I peeked through her window and girl why she had this big ass ugly white man half naked in the middle of her bedroom floor. I must've scared him when I knocked on the front door because he had started putting his clothes back on. I guess he thought I was her boyfriend or something judging by how nervous he was. My heart was beating a hundred miles a minute. I wanted to climb through that window and kick her ass, but decided not to. But I did bust out some of her fucking windows and cursed her ass till my mouth got tired."

"Max how many times must I tell you to leave those confused, wanna-be-gay one day and straight the next, chicken heads alone? You'll learn one day sweetie; the hard way nonetheless, but you'll learn. Shit…I can't really talk huh?"

"No, not really Dee…"

Yawning, I showed empathy towards my best friend's situation by asking her if she was OK. After she confirmed that she was alright, I suggested that we both turn in and get some much needed sleep.

"Wait a minute. Why are you rushing me off the phone Ms. Danielle Cyrus? You've been tired before and stayed on the phone with me. What's so special about tonight?"

"Nothing, I'm just getting up early to go running with Lexy." I said to her.

"Oh, so you're still dealing with her huh? I thought you left that alone because you felt bad about cheating on Malik again?"

"Yeah, I did. But then I thought about it and realized how stupid I was being. Malik's a married man. He sleeps with another woman every night and selfishly gets pussy from her and me. So, why in the hell should I feel bad about getting me some extra good-good on the side? Shit, I wish he would confront me about Lexy, or anybody else I choose to sleep with; that is should he ever find out."

"Touché," she cosigned on my epiphany.

Finally with Max's approval, we ended our late night Dr. Phil session. But once again guilt consumed me. I was keeping yet another secret from Malik. Thoughts of telling him about Lexy ran through my mind as I laid there in the dark, staring up at the ceiling, waiting to drift off to sleep. Lexy and I had been dating for some time now, and she had become an important part of my life. The secrecy of it all weighed heavily on my heart.

After how I treated Ariel, I refused to do that same thing to Lexy. But I knew Malik would never understand or approve of my involvement with her. He lived by such double standards. As long as he was the only one being allowed to sleep with someone else, everything was copacetic. Because people only did to you what you allowed them to, I guess Malik's actions were justified to some extent. And since I wasn't ready to risk my relationship with him just yet, I kept my relationship with Lexy private for the time being.

Chapter Seven

Ending my romance with Ariel was one of the hardest things I ever had to do. Being deceitful was not a trait I wanted to adopt, so I tried focusing solely on my relationship with Malik. I even went as far as to cancel my page on *Blackplanet* in an attempt to cleanse myself of women all together. I tried to convince myself that a gay lifestyle was not for me; I was a straight woman who went the extra mile one night for her man, that's all. Danielle Cyrus was not a lesbian!

Day after day and week after week I fought hard to deny my sexual longings for women, but the cravings were too strong. I couldn't ignore them anymore. Then one night, completely submissive to my emotions, I called Max to confess all that I had been hiding from her and everyone else. Happily, she insisted we go out to the gay club to celebrate. I was a little reluctant at first. The thought of being surrounded by nothing but gay women kind of freaked me out. Then at the same time it kind of turned me on. Weird....

That was the night I met Lexy. Personally, I had never intended for her to stick around. Hell, I had just come out of the closet and wanted to explore all my available options. The last thing I needed was to have a woman fall for me, or worse, me fall for her. But in life we learn that things don't always go as planned. So here it was three months later, and I'd managed to do exactly what I wasn't suppose to do; fall for another woman again. *Chaos!*

Beep…beep…beep… The alarm sounded. It was 7:00 A.M. and Lexy was expected to arrive at any minute. That damn Maxine and all her late night dramatics, I cursed as I jumped out of bed and darted towards the shower. My body was so tired, but I knew I had to get it together before she arrived. Thanks to Kelly Price playing in my CD player, a fresh pot of coffee brewing, and a hot shower, I would be revitalized in no time.

The water was scorching hot just the way I liked it. Standing there completely naked, I thought about Lexy as I slid my hands all over my body imagining my touches were hers. With the soapy washcloth I rubbed my skin in soft circular motions and allowed the excitement to blanket my body from the inside out. The rag grazed across my hardened nipples, and I pretended it was Lexy nibbling at my breast. With parted legs I welcomed the friction from the wash cloth as it lightly scraped across my now throbbing pussy; teasing my clit just enough to arouse it. "Ooh…" I moaned. Steadily massaging my kitty, I imagined it was Lexy's tongue gliding across my enlarged clitoris.

Ring…ring... My masturbation was rudely interrupted by the sound of the phone. Lexy had arrived and my horny ass was still in the shower getting my freak on.

Rushed, I stepped out of the shower. Grabbing my towel, I dove onto the bed and picked up the receiver. "Good morning beautiful," Lexy sang.

"Good morning," I replied.

"Ready yet?"

"Give me five-ten more minutes to finish getting dressed."

"Okay, no problem," she agreed. "I'm downstairs waiting when you're done."

I hung up the phone and rushed to my closet. I wanted to wear something extra tight-fitting. Something that looked painted onto my skin, something that left nothing to the imagination. Then I remembered buying a black two-piece stretch outfit, where the top was two sizes too small and the bottom didn't have enough material to be considered shorts-it was perfect! With sex still fresh on my mind, I wanted to tease my baby. I threw on my clothes in record time; eight minutes flat. I was ready!

Lexy stood patiently waiting; checking me out as I walked downstairs. Naturally, I acted like I didn't see her. I didn't want her to see me blush. I wanted to maintain my serious, yet sexy look. And as always she looked stunning even early in the morning. Her gray and white Reebok jogging suit coordinated well with her matching running shoes. A quick embrace by the already ajar passenger side door, once inside the car the door shut behind me.

A gentle woman was what I called her. Although very feminine on the surface, she always insisted on opening and closing doors for me; saying that a woman should always be catered to and acknowledged as a woman. Chivalry was alive and well as far as Lexy was concerned. She would always pull my chair out at the dinner table and be insulted if I reached to pay for the check. And unlike Malik, she made sure to walk me to my front door whenever she wasn't spending the night.

Lexy's beauty was undeniable; a perfect blend of characteristics from her Puerto Rican mother and her Jamaican father. Hell this was Miami, so half breeds came a dime a dozen. Most of Miami's population was either mixed or of Hispanic decent. I wasn't complaining. I loved having variety within one individual. Her long black curly hair which she often kept in a pony tail extended down the center of her back. When she moved it resembled deep synchronized ocean waves. Her skin was effortlessly smooth, perfectly bronzed, and without any flaws. She was gorgeous without being high maintenance. Bi-weekly nail touch ups and hair do's were not on her list of priorities. However, she did keep her feet soft and well manicured. Physically, she was phenomenal. Her athletic build was tightly packed and well proportioned within her tight 5'6" frame. Yeah, she was very pleasing to the eye.

Driving up the coast of Ft. Lauderdale Beach where the ocean breeze was always cool and the waves were always inviting, it was about 72 degrees, low humidity, and a perfect day for running. Scanning the beach we saw a few others also taking advantage of such a beautiful morning. Some people were nestled within their lover's arms watching as the sun rose lighting the earth's hemisphere. While others were walking hand in hand along the shoreline. And there were a small number of pedestrians getting in an early workout like me and Lexy. I for one loved the coast; there was nothing like it in the world. Whenever I needed to clear my head or escape my cluttered reality, the ocean was always my own personal sanctuary.

Before we actually began running, we did some simple stretches to warm our bodies up and after about ten minutes of that, we were ready. Lightly jogging first, and then gradually picking up the pace. Lexy was always at least two steps ahead of me, but that never stopped me from going. I cherished every moment I was allotted with her. Besides, I didn't mind the view from behind. Watching as her ass danced just for me with every step she took was enough motivation for me to keep up as best I could...*It must be jelly because jam don't shake like that,* I giggled to myself.

An hour had passed before we were back at the car. I was breathing like a dragon and sweating profusely. Lexy on the other hand, looked just as fresh and untouched as she did before we started. Our sixty minutes of running was nothing compared to her usual workout routine. She always shortened the distance of her runs whenever I tagged along to compensate for my athletic handicap, I was grateful for that.

Starving, I insisted we grab some breakfast. After that workout I had a man-sized appetite, so we stopped into our usual spot for a bite to eat. It was a small yet, classy little café. Lexy liked it because they specialized in healthy natural breakfast shakes and meals. Being as health conscious as she was, she refused to eat any solids after a vigorous morning workout; that was her hang up not mine. Usually, I'd humor her by getting a health shake along with a fruit plate, and then once I got home, I would make pancakes, sausage, and eggs. Today was different. I was starving. I had to get a little more than the usual, so I ordered a blueberry muffin and a side order of turkey bacon to go along with my fruit and shake. Hey, I ran hard and deserved a treat.

"Thirsty boo?" I asked Lexy after she gulped down her shake like it was her first meal in days. Looking at her empty glass smiling, "Yeah a little… are we still having dinner tonight?" Oh shit! I had forgotten about my plans with her. Malik and I were supposed to meet up for drinks and a movie later. I had to think fast on my feet. "Oh baby, I completely forgot about tonight. I'm sorry. Maxine called late last night with her usual drama and asked me to come over tonight. She needs a kind shoulder to cry on and being that I am worried about her present state of mind, I told her I would. Poor girl was dumped again last night and sounded really horrible." I lied. "But I can call her and tell her I'd come by first thing tomorrow instead."

"No…no, that's your best friend and I'd be mad at you if you didn't go to console her. We can hang out another time; don't worry about it."

"Are you sure?" I asked.

"Of course, I'm sure."

"Thanks babe! You're too good to me." I leaned in to kiss her.

Believe it or not, I hated lying to her. She was too good a person and deserved more than what I was giving, but I was too selfish to let her go. I'll get my shit together some day. I just hope it's sooner than later because tomorrows not always promised to you.

Chapter Eight

After our meal we went back to my condo to freshen up. The fact that I had just lied to her had me feeling awfully needy. I wanted to be close to her and I didn't want her to walk away from me empty as well. The thought of touching her soft caramelized skin hastily provoked feelings of intimacy. I wondered if she would be up for a quickie before she left for work.

Apparently, Lexy felt the need for some intimacy as well. Soon as the door closed shut, she grabbed a hold of me from behind. Her slender arms wrapped around my waist and with gentle maneuvers she kissed along the back of my neck.

She must've had the same kind of shower I had earlier this morning, I thought to myself. Turning to face her, I removed the out of place hairs from her face, so I could look into her big beautiful dark brown eyes. Her lips were slightly wet from where she had previously licked and kissed up and down the spine of my neck. Lexy knew that kissing was my most favorite part of foreplay; therefore, she did not hesitate to shove her tongue deep inside my mouth, penetrating the nerves to my pussy.

It didn't take long for us to be all over each other once inside the house. Caught up in the moment we touched, grabbed, and squeezed any and everything our hands came into contact with. Stumbling and falling onto the sofa, damn near missing it, we never interrupted our flow. Unstoppable and driven by pure lust, we were like that damn rabbit from the Energizer Battery commercials...we kept going and going and going.

"Oho...baby you feel so good, but let's take a shower first," she insisted as she led me to the bathroom. Wanting to go all the way at that moment, I thought better of it. We both had just finished running, and there were places on our bodies that seriously needed the attention of some soap and water. I loved women, true, but it came a point when as a woman I knew when to stop and freshen up.

Inside the shower we took turns washing each other; paying particular attention to the common areas that we planned to share soon after. Lexy had the prettiest pussy I had ever seen, no lie. It was always so nicely groomed, never a single hair out of place. The folds of her vulva skin were virgin tight and her clit maintained stamina as if she kept a 24-hour hard on. A perfect mirage of purity, but she was far from virginal. I knew someone had to have frequented there, at least once, during her heterosexual lifetime.

Call me weird, but sometimes I would sit unbeknownst to her, and stare aimlessly at her pussy while she slept. I just loved being near it. I loved kissing it. I even loved the smell of it. How is it that I was so sure of how I felt about her snatch, but so unsure of how I felt about her…past the intimacy? I knew I cared a lot about her, I just didn't know if I could honestly say I loved her.

Exiting the shower, still intertwined, we found ourselves on the bed. Hands firm behind my back, Lexy laid me down in such a gentle manner. It was as if she thought she'd break me if she weren't careful. Little things like that were why I adored her and women in general. Compared to men, women were much gentler and passionate when it came to their partner. And it was no secret that Lexy loved the hell out of my yellow ass.

Taking her rightful place, she began grinding on top of me; causing our pussies to rub savagely against one another. Saturated, I felt her moisture drizzle down my thighs onto my legs. Feeling the heat from her exerted pussy served as an aphrodisiac, heightening my sexual tendencies to a whole nother degree. Back and forth…back and forth… with so much passion; had she had a dick - which I often wished she did - she would've fucked the shit out of me. Sexually, Lexy was a stallion; she possessed the power to keep me in a submissive trance. Sex with her often minimized Malik's efforts thereafter, so why was I not exclusively hers? That question still remained.

"Damn baby, slow down. You're about to make me cum," I pleaded with her as I bit down on my bottom lip, while gripping her by the ass.

"Feels good baby?" she asked as if she didn't already know the answer.

"Hell yeah," I screamed! Fighting the urge to buck like a horse underneath her, I tried to think of any and everything else to keep from cumming. I was loosing miserably, I watched as her titties bounced up and down as she rode me, penetrating my kitty. Eyes closed shut; I pressed and pulled her harder against my clit, signaling to my orgasmic missiles that it was time for take off. With the count down in full affect 5, 4, 3, 2, 1... my insides exploded like fireworks on Independence Day. Once the celebration was over, simultaneously, we both exhaled and collapsed on the bed. I wanted to lie there for a minute; just long enough to catch my breath before flipping her onto her back, but before I could make a move, she got up and headed toward the bathroom.

"Where are you going?" I asked a little confused.

"I have to get to the hospital. I'm on call today. I just wanted to break my baby off before I went to work. One must take care of home first right?" With a kiss to the forehead, she took a quick wash off ahead of getting dressed.

I knew it would be days before I saw her again. I wanted to kick my feet and pout like a baby in an attempt to keep her home. Yes, I was having one of my spoiled brat moments. I wanted to keep her to myself for a little while longer. Work was important to her and I knew that, but I couldn't help but feel sad.

Lexy's work as a RN for *Aventura Hospital* in North Miami kept her schedule hectic on any given day. She typically worked 12-16 hours a day, three to four days a week. In her off time she still remained on call in case of emergencies. Unfortunately, there was always an emergency, i.e. like right now. This allowed no real personal time for us; hence, I was left alone more often than not. That was the main reason I continued to fuck with Malik. Married or not, he always had time for me and I needed someone with time.

Lexy finished getting dressed and I walked her to the door. Sorrow took my joy as we kissed goodbye. Turning to walk away, she looked back to tell me she loved me and without waiting for a response, her back became my only view. I was use to this type of abrupt departure from her. I think Lexy knew I wasn't in love with her, which explained why she never waited or expected a response from me whenever she told me she loved me. *"Smart girl…Very smart girl,"* I thought. She chose to protect her heart by not knowing.

Truthfully I wanted to be in love with her, but most of our encounters ended abruptly like this. The inconsistency within our relationship kept my feelings for her from evolving to a deeper level. Besides the physical attraction, I wasn't exactly sure how I felt about her.

Whoever said absence made the heart grow fonder bluntly lied. Absence, in my opinion, allowed space and opportunity for someone else to pick up where your lover left off. Our relationship was still fairly new, and it lacked nurturing. A flower can't bloom without proper care and Lexy was unavailable a lot. To sum up our relationship in a nutshell, we were like associates with excellent benefits.

Chapter Nine

It was still early when I decided to call Max to see if she wanted to hang out. "Hey girl," she answered.

"What's up?"

"Nothing much; wanted to see if you felt like hanging this afternoon?"

"Let me guess, your oochie coochie was cut short today," she teased. "You know that you never call me after a morning run with Lexy. Usually you're too tied up - literally.

"Look slut you going to chill with me or not? Lexy had to work today, but don't act like I only call you when she's not available."

"No, you call when Malik's not available too," she laughed.

"Look bitch I will be to your house around 4 P.M. so be ready."

"Okay, where we going?"

"I feel like seeing some ass. How you feel about the strip club?"

"Shit, you know I'm always down for seeing Carmen."

"You still stuck on that girl? I really need you to broaden your horizon a little Max. There are plenty of other girls up in there for you to drool over. Get off Carmen titties already."

"I ain't on em yet," she teased.

"Girl, get off my phone. I'll see you in a few."

We got off the phone and I went to freshen up. Normally, I wouldn't go to strip clubs, but desperate times called for desperate measures and I needed more. Lexy had left me horny and unsatisfied. I still longed to be in the company of a woman. Preferably her company, but the girls down at the strip club would have to do for now.

The Pink Pony was packed for it to still be so early in the evening. I insisted on going during the off peak hours because it was less crowded and the women seemed to pay us lesbians more attention. Prime time evening hours were when the dancers would downplay their natural instincts by seeming uninterested in dancing for female spectators. Shit that was their loss. We lesbians were the better tippers anyway.

Amongst the fakers were a few true to the core lesbians that would only dance for the ladies, but there were far more dick dykes, who feared that if they solely danced for women, they would jeopardize their tips from the male clientele. I ain't mad at them though. This was all a hustle and may the best bitch win in my opinion.

Carmen's sexy ass noticed Max as soon as we walked through the door. Like a moth to a flame, she attached herself to Max's wallet…I meant Maxine. Carmen was nobody's fool. She was smart. There was a method to her madness. She knew Max loved the hell out of her performance, so she attached herself to Max well before any of the other women could. Many times in the past, Max had blown well over $500 dollars on just her during one sitting. Max could be so gullible at times, especially around a clique of naked clits. Sometimes I wondered if she knew it was all a mind fuck; nothing more…nothing less. These girls could care less about her. Paper chasing was the name of the game and all the girls were constantly trying to stay in the lead.

The scents of cucumber melons, cotton candy, and vanilla musk aggressively commandeered the club's stale atmosphere. It wasn't as dark as I would've liked for it be. Not to be mean, but some chicks look much better under dimmed lights.

Girls, girls, and more girls of all nationalities were walking about with little to nothing on. Some light skinned, some dark skinned, some pretty, and some just damn right ugly. Fortunately for me, most of the dancers were faceless. Any physical features above the neckline didn't matter to me. Purposely avoiding eye contact, I probably wouldn't be able to identify anyone of them on the streets, if I ever bumped into them.

It was interesting to watch the different interactions from across the small dark room. Everyone had their type. Me, I preferred those high yella, biracial women. Something about them drove me crazy. Everything about them was intriguing to me, from their smooth baby soft skin, to their highly opinionated personas. Add in the feisty attitudes, which I loved, and you have yourself the perfect blend of trouble.

Inside the small claustrophobic club was plenty of empty seats since it were still early. Next to the stage, I found a nice spot to plant myself. Max was already missing in action; probably getting her first of many lap dances in their overpriced champagne room, a.k.a. a small booth hidden behind polyester curtains. And like bees to honey, they migrated in her direction. Max was none-the wiser, or at least she acted that way. I didn't want to spoil her fun, so I sat idly by while she enjoyed her evening.

Getting lap dances wasn't really my thing. I enjoyed sitting up front admiring the performers on stage, but that's about it. Simulated fucks were pointless to me. After being dry humped for two minutes, then what? Then if you want more time with the dancer, it'll cost you another $5-10 bucks for another two minutes. No, I took great pleasure in watching the stunts being performed on stage, rather than having someone bend over aimlessly in front of me; leaving only her ass crack for my viewing pleasure.

Above the petite square shaped stage sat the DJ overlooking the club. His job was to keep everybody in the building crunk, spiraling down from the dancers to the sponsors of the dancers. He was doing his job well. Each time a dancer passed by a man, he would yell out over the mic for him to tip the pretty lady.

"Aight fellas, these ladies work hard for their money and they should be tipped appropriately. If you want to look at naked ass for free, then the strip club ain't the place for you to be."

As I looked around the club one thing came to mind, the movie Players Club. The vibe and the décor were a precise match. Booty shaking music thumped loudly from the speakers located directly in front of the stage, as herds of women paraded up and down the floor. They were persistent and offered lap dances to whomever made eye contact with them. For that reason alone I made sure to always keep my focus to the stage. That way my only obligation was to the women on stage and not the ones walking around.

After a few hours had passed, several performances, three Long Island Ice Teas, and me making it rain on the stage, I was ready to call it quits. It was Sunday and I did have to go to work the next day. Just as I stood up to get Max's attention, the DJ announced, "Coming to the stage for your viewing pleasure, the sexy, the naughty, the tameless…please welcome Ms. Lollipop."

Convinced that I had seen enough, I wasn't trying to turn around, but something told me I had to. When I did, my knees gave way beneath me. This woman was amazing! She was much too beautiful of a creature to be caught up in this type of life style. She stood about 5'7", model frame, not anorexic, but a good healthy weight. Fair skinned, with tattooed paws leading up to her lady zone. Captivated by her eyes, it seemed as if she focused all her attention right in my direction. Like lion hunting his next prey, she crouched down on all fours (so sexy) and crawled towards the end of the stage where I stood.

Barely dressed in a sheer white baby doll teddy, I admired her curves and the slow seductive sway of her hips, as she made her way down the short, but particularly lengthy stage at that moment. Watching this alluring woman crawl on her hands and knees to me was a real live fantasy. There was a certain thirst in her approach, indicating to me that I was the only one capable of quenching it. Envious glares pierced the back of my neck as everyone watched this seductive mistress float my way.

Flirtatious and sexy with it, she smiled as she reached the end of the stage where I stood frozen. This had to be how Carmen made Max feel. The seductive professional tricked me into believing that this was all real. I started to feel like she was there just for me. I finally understood how a person could get caught up and completely forget that it was all make believe.

"Hey beautiful," she said, as she opened wide to wrap her long legs around my waist. Grinning devilishly, "You like what you see don't you?"

"Yes… I do, very much so." I confidently replied reaching for my pockets to tip her.

"No sweetheart, put that back. This one is on me." Pulling me closer into her, she made sure we connected pelvis to pelvis. Background fading, music barely above a whisper, I was lost in her world.

With her mouth close to my ear, the sweetest moans escaped her lips with every grind of her eager hips. Rubbing up my back, underneath my shirt, goose bumps crept up along the areas where she had previously traced with her finger tips. My hardened nipples were apparent, she teased at them with the tip of her nose. There was no doubt about it, this chick was mind fucking the hell out of me and wanted to make sure I received the message loud and clear.

The end of the song approached, and I can't lie, I wasn't ready for it to be over. My panties were soaked, my clit was hurting, and my body seriously needed some relief before I ruptured. Between what had transpired with Lexy earlier, and now this, oh I was going to relieve myself one way or the other.

"Thanks for the dance sweet face," she said as the song ended. "By the way, I like what I see as well." Then she kissed my cheek and made her rounds around the stage. From the soft touch of her lips against my cheek, there was a sudden release of pressure…an orgasmic relief. I've cum from kissing Lexy in the heat of the moment, I've even cum from eating Ariel's pussy, but to cum from a stranger

71

dancing for me was unconceivable. I wasn't sure if that had just happened, but whatever it was left me completely content.

Pure in my thoughts, I didn't care to see the rest of my mystery woman's performance. I wanted to hold on to that experience for as long I could without contamination. I didn't want to think about the reality of it; she was a stripper and did this every night for different people. However, tonight, I claimed the fantasy that I was her one and only.

Max and I left the club around 9 P.M. I was ready to go home, take a hot shower, and think more about Ms. Lollipop.

"So, I see you have an admirer…" Max teased.

"Yeah I guess I do," I smiled back at her.

"She was nice Dee…"

"Yes, she was!"

"I think she liked you too." Maxine suggested.

"Nah, she was just performing. Probably gave it to me free as a form of paying it forward; a deposit if you will, hoping that I'd come back as a regular." I said this trying to convince myself that it was a dance and nothing more.

"I don't know…I don't know." Max said, as she laid her head on the headrest staring out the window.

Truthfully I thought she liked me too, but I had to know better of it. Last thing I needed was to end up sprung out on some stripper like Max. I had way too much baggage already and didn't need to add someone else to my special blend of chaos. The girl was beautiful, and under different circumstances I may have wanted to get to know her better, but at present day, I had to pass.

Thoughts of Ms. Lollipop's paw trail tattoo ran through my mind all the way home. Its location was appealing and aroused my curiosity about what happens once you reached the end of the paw trail. "T- Pain" said it best with his hit song I'm in love with a stripper. OK, so I wasn't in love with a stripper per se, but I was damn sure infatuated with one. I had to get her out of my head. Picking up my phone, I called my girlfriend, then Malik to bring me back to my reality.

Chapter Ten

Monday morning, the weekend had flown by so fast. It was time to deal with the pressures of the real world. Traffic, road rage, and begging ass roadside vagrants; too damn lazy to go out and get a job. They'd prefer to beg for money on the street corner versus trying to do better for themselves. In fairness, I understood that some people were just born into a rough life, but I also knew that some of those same people just needed help. It was hard to distinguish just by looking at them, which was which.

Hurriedly, I struggled to get dressed. My mind raced with hopes of leaving the house thirty minutes earlier than usual, as I tried to beat the 7:00 A.M. traffic rush on I-95. Once in my car, I tuned in to my favorite radio station "Power 96." The combination of the morning DJ mixed with caffeine always pumped me up, and I really needed that extra boost of energy today.

During my drive to work, constant thoughts of Malik and how *most* times I enjoyed being with him, replayed over and over again in my mind. Together, we really had some great times. I loved his steadfast business personality and even more, his covert silly side. Often times, I would close my eyes and pretend for an instant that I was Mrs. Malik Michaels. A fair part of me wished that Malik solely belonged to me, but I knew the rules going in.

His marriage was no secret. In the beginning, I really thought my skin was tough enough to handle sharing him. But as we all know, your heart doesn't always do what your mind tells it to. So, there I was, hopelessly in love with a married man who I knew was on borrowed time and could never officially be mine.

My thoughts for the morning were interrupted by my early arrival to the parking garage of my office building. Slightly halting before getting out of my car, I said a quick prayer just as I always did before starting my workday. This was not a negative ritual, but a necessary one. I knew the stresses of my job and I knew nothing positive would come out of today, or the next four days to be exact. Working as an advertising executive, at one of "Miami's" most prestigious advertising firms, my days were compiled with endless deadlines, bottomless cups of office coffee, and stuck-up snobbish CEOs and Vice-Presidents. With the stress of my high-paced career, and now the increasing stress of my ever unstable social life, it was a miracle I hadn't gone postal yet…emphasis on yet.

"Good morning Ms. Cyrus," said my Administrative Assistant, Ms. Jenkins, as I walked past her desk.

"Good morning Ms. Jenkins. Has the portfolio I requested from the "Nike" accounts come in yet?"

"No, not yet; I'm working on that as we speak," she said with hesitation in her voice.

I responded with agitation, "Ms. Jenkins, I requested that portfolio from you last week, and now my patience has grown thin. If I don't get that portfolio by Wednesday, you may want to consider another place of employment." I gave her a stern look to emphasize the seriousness of the situation and slammed my office door behind me, co-signing my intent.

She's my assistant, and her job was to assist me. She had become way too complacent and had mistaken my kindness for weakness. I had to put things back into perspective for her and let her know that when I request information about an important account, I am going to need her to make that a priority. Of course, once I was behind closed doors, I admitted to myself that my actions were like that of a true bitch and that maybe I over reacted. My momma did raise me better than that. So no matter what my issues, I shouldn't have spoken to her in that manner. I promised myself to apologize to her later. Stressed out as usual...

Monday had finally come to an end. After smoothing things over with Ms. Jenkins, without taking away from the point I was trying to make, I needed an escape in the form of an alcoholic beverage. A liquid cure-all and I knew exactly where to go to get it.

Jay's parking lot was fairly empty around 6:00 P.M. when I arrived. Seeing that it was only Monday, and still early, I wasn't surprised. Most people in Miami didn't come out until the sun had gone completely down, which didn't bother me. Less people inside the bar, meant less people to deal with. I could drink undisturbed, grab some finger food, and then go home.

Jay's was one of the few gay establishments in Miami/Ft. Lauderdale. A bar by day and a dance club by night. I first found out about this place the night I came out of the closet to Maxine. It was extremely small in size, but to my surprise it had two bars, a few tables with chairs, and a stage for performances. *Jay's* replicated the typical sports bar. Pool tables were to the right side of the bar, neon rainbow colored lights hung from the cracked walls, and a few slot machines sat horizontally on each bar.

Seating apparently was not a priority, due to the lack of chairs throughout the building. And the cooling system needed a little work, which became evident during the crowded club nights. But overall it was a decent place, serving its purpose. Thinking back to when Max first brought me to *Jay's*, I was so apprehensive. But if she hadn't convinced me to come, I would've never met Lexy. Before then, I hadn't ever stepped foot instead a gay club before. I was in an utter state of shock. There were women that looked like men, and men that looked liked women. I was so confused.

****

The club was packed from wall to wall. Maxine reminded me that there weren't many gay clubs in Miami and that was why it was so crowded. Like a fish out of water I was panicking. Eyes from every angle of the room darted in my direction. It was as if I looked different from everyone else or something. Or, maybe, it was just that I was a newbie surrounded by all the weekly regulars. Whatever the reason it didn't change the fact that I felt like raw meat in the midst of a pack of hungry wolves.

As we pushed our way through the congested crowd, I chuckled at the numerous times my ass was molested. It was flattering, but at the same time nerve wrecking. The mannerisms of some women were much like men, if not worse. Needless to say, I clung to Maxine like white on rice. Although I was charmed by the attention the women were giving me, I was still too new to the lifestyle to be walking around solo.

Isolated in a tiny corner by one of the jukeboxes, I sipped my fourth Long Island Ice Tea and that's when my night took a drastic turn. Loose as a goose, all my inhibitions were lost; I transformed from timid and reserved, to obnoxiously wild and tasteless. Assuming ownership of the crowded dance floor, I danced all night with all kinds of women: fat women, skinny women, pretty women, even ugly women. I didn't discriminate against anyone that night. No one wore a face. Through my drunken eyes everybody looked like "America's Next Top Model."

Then suddenly out of nowhere, someone reached through the crowd, taking me by force as they led me to an open space away from the crowded room. I couldn't make out her face, but from the back, baby was thick as hell. Once in a secluded area the stranger wiped the sweat from my brow and fanned me in an attempt to cool me off.

In a maternal voice, "Are you alright sweetie?" she asked, while handing me a bottle of water.

"I'm fine!" I snapped, taking the water from her hand. Insulted by her actions, I asked her name.

"My name is Alexis Roberts, but you can call me Lexy."

Reluctantly, I offered my name, "Danielle Cyrus, nice to meet you." My attitude was a lil' catty I admit, but who did she think she was…my woman? Snatching me off the damn dance floor like that, she lucky I didn't slap the shit out of her for that. However, I was thankful for the bottle of water.

"Look at me Danielle." Lexy gently palmed my face. "I want to look into your eyes to make sure you're alright." Was this the best pick up line she could think of? I chuckled to myself. Humoring her, I looked up not anticipating such a beauty. One look into her big beautiful eyes, and I became filled with shame for my behavior. Completely cognizant of my floozy-like actions on the dance floor, I hung my head low out of embarrassment. Dancing on all those women was not lady-like at all. I had never been so disappointed in myself in my whole life. Oddly, Lexy didn't seem to mind.

"I like the way you moved out there," she said through a wicked smirk. I wasn't sure what to think of her, or that comment. Was she looking for a one night stand? I asked myself. Her sincerity towards me didn't exemplify that at all. She seemed to be more concerned with my overall well being vs. what was in my panties.

Staying by my side, she continued to wipe the sweat from my brow. Making sure I stayed well hydrated. I should've known then that she was a medical professional. A true lover of one's career is always on duty; whether they are on or off the clock. Her natural instincts had stepped in and took its course. And for the remainder of that night, I belonged to Lexy with absolutely no regrets.

****

"Excuse me." My thoughts were intruded upon when a burly woman offered to buy me a drink. Respectively, I declined her offer. I quickly paid my tab and got the hell out of dodge. Last thing I needed was a woman who was manlier than Malik.

Hair to the wind…I left the bar. Once in my car, I called Maxine to see what she was up to. No answer, so I left a message.

"Hey Max, it's me Danielle. I was just calling to see if you wanted to catch a movie tonight. Call me when you get this message."

Hanging up, I tried calling Malik next, but to no avail. Where the hell is everyone? I thought to myself, as I pulled into the drive thru of Pollo Tropical to get some dinner.

"May I take your order?" the young girl announced through the microphone.

"Yes, I would like a quarter chicken value meal and a side order of plantains."

"Your total is $5.60. Drive up to the first window please."

At the window, I paid the adolescent who was sporting dark blue and bright red braids. I swear some things were only acceptable in Miami. Starving, that food smelled so damn good I couldn't wait to get home and fuck it up.

Reaching my home, my stomach growled as I walked through the front door. Then my cell phone started ringing. Pressing the "END" button, I sent it straight to voicemail. Whoever it was just had to wait; I was too hungry to stop and engage in any type of casual conversation.

Chapter Eleven

Coming home to my condo in North Lauderdale was always relaxing after a long hard day. Not very many black people lived in my community, which tended to keep the crime rate down to pretty much non-existent. Obsessively finicky about my place of residence, I was very pleased to see that the property was well maintained and my neighbors were genuinely friendly.

Now don't get me wrong, I love my black people, but y'all know how we are when it's too many of us in a secluded area. Property value gradually goes down, late night loud house parties, and don't forget about the infamous bad-ass rug rats running around tearing shit up. Kids seemed to have the gift of destroying nice places from within. And the noise levels, forget about it, sleepless nights were definite.

Appreciative that I sprung for the building with zero-tolerance for kids and gangsters, I plotted down directly in front of my ridiculously large 60" flat screen TV, and ate my dinner. Devouring my meal so fast, I'm sure I forgot to chew a couple of times. Minutes after I was done eating, I found myself in the bathroom hurled over the toilet. I had to have eaten a bad piece of chicken, or had a small case of acid reflux. *Damn, I hope I don't have food poisoning, but if I do, I'm gon' sue the hell out of Pollo Tropical,* I thought in between barfs.

Since I ate there at least three times a week, I doubted it was food poisoning. Guess it's a first time for everything. Ugh! My stomach was boiling. Feeble, I decided to lie down for a while until the room stopped spinning.

Ring…, ring…, my phone. "Hello," I answered.

"Danielle, I know you ain't sleeping," Maxine yelled in my ear.

"Lower your damn voice. I'm not feeling well."

"Oh, I'm sorry honey. What's wrong?"

"I think I had some bad chicken from the restaurant. I'm gon' holla at you later," I said, as I hung the phone up without waiting for a response.

Not one for rejection, Max drove straight to my house after I hung up on her. Twenty minutes tops and she was at my gatehouse, buzzing for me to let her in. Hesitant, I allowed her access by pressing the star key on the phone pad. It was times like this that made me happy she had a key to my place, to let herself in. I was way too weak to leave my bed.

"Max what are you doing here?" I whined.

"You hang up in my face and expect me to accept that? You should know better than that Dee…What's ailing you anyway?"

"My stomach is killing me. Feels like I had one too many drinks, but worse. Pass me the wastebasket in case I can't make it to the bathroom. And will you grab me a glass of water please?" In sync with my needs, Max did not hesitate to assist me. She did exactly as I asked of her. That was one of the many things I loved about her. She was always there for me, whether I wanted her to be or not.

Unsurprisingly, Max stayed the night with me, gently rubbing my head until I fell asleep. Stubborn as she was, she was also equally loyal. I hated to admit it, but I was glad she came over. I hadn't realized how much I needed her until she was there by my side, making sure I was OK, like a best friend should.

Sun light shown through the partially separated wooden blinds, and my Max was still there. Actually, she was in the kitchen cooking. Normally, I would've loved to have been served breakfast in bed, but not today. "Good morning sunshine, are you feeling better?" Maxine sang. I tried to respond, but the smell of bacon and eggs sent my stomach in an uproar. Nearly knocking Max off her feet, I ran towards the bathroom.

"Danielle, if I didn't know any better, I would think you were pregnant."

"That's ridiculous. Malik and I use protection," I said defensively, as soon I managed to speak without regurgitating.

"All the time?" she quizzed.

Thinking, "Most of the time," I responded with less aggression in my tone.

"I have a pregnancy test at home that I could go get, and then we can squash this ridiculous assumption of mine, as you so eloquently put it." She offered.

"Nah, I'm good, but what the hell are you doing with a pregnancy test?" Reversing the interrogation towards her, "I thought I was the only one who straddled the fence."

"This ain't about me Danielle. I'm not the one questioning my sudden illness." Maxine said as she quickly gathered her belongings. She hated when I reversed a situation around on her, putting her in the hot seat.

"I love you Dee, but I gotta go. I'm done with my nurturing duties for today. Talk to you later. But seriously call me if you need me, and please take a test. If not for you, then do it for me." She kissed my cheek and left for work.

The thought of being pregnant never entered my mind; although, this was the first time I had missed my period in 14 years. Glad I left that part out of my conversation with Maxine. Last thing I needed was to fuel her comical accusations. Otherwise, she would've never left. She probably would've gone out and started shopping for the kid before the pregnancy was ever confirmed. No, I think I'll keep that little fact to myself, at least until I knew for sure.

Wow! If I was pregnant, telling Malik would not be an option. He was already married with a kid. Having a baby out of wedlock was not in my life's plan or his. Matter of fact, children were not in my life's plan at all! It was bad enough that I was a bisexual woman fucking a married man, along with another woman on the side, and neither one of them knew of the other person. But to bring forth a baby from this tangled web of lies I called a life, would be wrong. My mother and grandmother would turn twice over in their graves, if I purposely wronged a child like that. Regardless of the outcome, I needed to know for sure. Feeling much better than I did the night prior, I convinced myself to go to Walgreens and buy a pregnancy test.

EPT, First Response, Clear Blue Easy, even a Walgreens brand. There were so many different brands to choose from. Which one should I choose? After reading the informational message on several boxes, I decided to go with EPT. It's supposed to be an error proof test…99.9% effective.

"Good luck!" The cashier said to me as she handed me my change.

"Hopefully not," I replied. Puzzled by my response her mouth hung open, as she watched me exit the store.

Without haste, I went home to take the test. Not only was the curiosity killing me, but also I had to pee like a race horse. Yep, miraculously, since this morning, I adopted all the alarming signs of pregnancy, in as little as one day. Scientists, believe that the mind is so powerful, that it can send false messages to the rest of the body making the body experience signs of illness even if it's not factual, i.e. hypochondriacs. So pregnancy symptoms weren't so farfetched.

Before starting the test, I made sure to read the instructions carefully ensuring that I took the test right the first time. I only had one applicator, so I had to be precise. The test said to wait three minutes after peeing on the white test strip, before reading the results. Setting the timer for three minutes, I waited very impatiently. Those had to have been the longest three minutes of my life. Ding…Time was up. My heart beat rapidly as the moment of truth arrived. Am I, or aren't I? Slowly, I walked towards the bathroom sink, breathing heavily almost to the point of hyperventilating. Test stick in my hand, I looked down to read the results… and – Pregnant! I screamed! The fucking test read pregnant!

Me…Danielle Ieshia Cyrus, pregnant - what was I going to do? My mind raced, my heart thumped dangerously fast, and tears fell from my eyes. My life as I knew it was ruined. Who was I kidding? I was in no position to be a mommy. I didn't even have a grip on my social affairs. How in the hell was I going take care of a baby? I can't even take care of myself properly most of the time. I needed to see Malik, so I called him.

"Hey baby." His masculine voice answered and calmed me all over.

"I need to see you," I demanded of him.

"What's wrong Dee?"

"I just really need to see you," I reiterated my initial statement.

"Okay, okay, I'm on my way. Sit still until I get there alright?"

"I will."

We hung up and I pondered over whether or not to tell him. I needed to think quickly. He'd be here in about 15 minutes. Being that he was still ignorant to the fact, abortion was an option; but what if he wanted the baby? What if he wanted a family with me and our unborn child? Yeah right. Reality kicked in. Mr. Michaels was not about to leave his trophy wife and well-maintained life for me, his confused-ass mistress.

Chapter Twelve

Malik arrived to my apartment approximately 15 minutes later. "Baby, you OK?" He asked very concerned like.

"I'm fine, now that you're here."

"You scared me Dee…what's up with you?" He asked, while embracing me.

"I'm sorry I made you worry. I just needed to see and feel you next to me. Hold me closer Malik; I need you to hold me closer." I begged of him, with tears running down my cheek onto his Hanes t-shirt. Judging by his attire, he left as soon as we hung up the phone. White t-shirt, baggy jeans, and sandals were not Malik's usual attire. He was strictly a suit and tie man, on all occasions.

His embrace was soothing; I was made to feel safe within his arms. My heart didn't have to question my feelings for him, unlike it did with Lexy. I loved Malik and there was no doubt about that. I wanted so much to have a family with him, but I knew he wouldn't approve of our baby. And that thought sliced through my heart like a hot knife through butter. How could I love someone that much, knowing that he would never be mine? Holding me close, looking down at me, Malik wiped the tears from my eyes. He knew something wasn't right, but didn't force me to talk.

I must've fallen asleep because two hours later I awoke in Malik's arms. Waking up to him like that reminded me of how I longed to wake up with him every day, but the reality of the situation was, this was as good as it was going get for me, on any given day. Sometimes I wished that he would've just walked right passed me that night we met, so long ago, rather than being as smooth as he was. Then maybe…just maybe, I wouldn't be in the predicament I was in right now; pregnant and in love with a married-cheating ass man. *Chaos!*

****

Like every good story, we too, have a beginning. The night we met was straight out of a storybook. It was a rainy June evening in hot Miami, Florida. The weather man had predicted a light shower, but nothing of this magnitude. I was on my way to meet Maxine for dinner at TGI Fridays, out in the well-manicured city of Aventura. The restaurant was located around the corner from where she was sponsoring a hair show.

Waiting to cross the street in front of the restaurant, a heavy gust of wind rushed by, and sent my umbrella flying in the air. Unfortunately for me, I did not have a back up plan. I was left standing in the rain, with my four –hundred-and-fifty dollar DKNY Pant suit, matching boots, and salon wrapped hair that was slowly starting to frizz up from the rain. Needless to say, I was soaked from head to toe and looked like a well-dressed poodle. And that's when Mr. Rico

Suave himself, appeared from nowhere to shelter me from the storm by way of his massive umbrella.

Malik was well groomed and dressed in an expensive, yet subtle, black Armani suit. The fragrance of his cologne signified masculinity without being obnoxious. Pretending to not be moved by his charitable gesture, or his intimidating stature, I thanked him for his help while deeply inhaling his scent. Weakened, I begged my knees not to go out on me. Without even knowing his name at the time, I had already become putty in this stranger's hands. What can I say; I've always been a sucker for a man with style and sex appeal. And Malik was batting two for two. He was the complete package.

Trying hard to snap out of the trace he had unknowingly put me under, I thanked him once more for sheltering me from the storm, and offered him my hand in gratitude. Taking it, he just smiled and asked where I was going, because he was willing to walk with me to keep me from getting wet. Huh, little did he know my hair and clothes weren't the only things wet at that moment.

Not wanting our acquaintance to end so soon, I told him that I was going to meet my best friend for dinner, and he was welcome to walk me the rest of the way. For the life of me, I couldn't quite understand why he was being such a gentlemen; especially when I knew I looked like a HAM... (Hot Ass Mess). Whatever his reasons that night, I didn't care. I was enjoying being in his presence, and eating up every allotted moment I had with him.

Outside the restaurant, I finally asked him his name. "Malik Michaels," he replied. "And you are?"

"My name is Danielle Cyrus, nice to meet you Mr. Michaels."

"Call me Malik, please."

"Okay, Malik. Thanks again for your help."

"No problem, Danielle. It is okay for me to call you that right?"

"Danielle is fine, or Dee, whichever you like." Hell I didn't care what he called me, as long as he called me.

"May I buy you a drink, while we await your friend?" Smiling girlishly, I accepted. "Yes, I would like that. I'll have a Long Island Ice Tea, thank you." Malik ordered our drinks, as we settled to a table. We talked for what seemed like hours, before I realized that Maxine hadn't called, or arrived yet. Reaching for my phone to check for messages, I noticed that I had one missed call and a text message. Per her text, she had called to cancel. She got held up at the hair show and couldn't make it to dinner. Not the least bit disappointed, I turned my focus back to my newly found interest. And what started out as a friendly gesture, was quickly re-routed into an awesome first date.

From the beginning, he was completely honest and up front about his marriage to Angela, and about their eight-year-old daughter, Jasmine. Not too many men would admit to being married with kids on a first date, so instantly he gained my utmost respect. I knew better then to entertain him after that revelation, but I was gone y'all; floating on cloud nine. It had been a long time since I had such an intense conversation with the opposite sex that I cherished every minute of it.

And in my delusional state of mind back then, I didn't want to face his reality. The ignorant side of me figured that there was no harm in getting a few free dinners, nice gifts, and possibly some great sex. If he was willing to step out on his family to be with me, or the next woman, then that's exactly what he was going to do. Hell, why not enjoy a free ride? He had as much of a hand in it as I did. Therefore, I ignored my inner voice, which was telling me to leave well enough alone, and sat, indulging myself in the company of Mr. Malik Michaels.

Months had passed and we started seeing more of each other regularly. He would come up with all kinds of brilliant excuses to tell his wife, and I would go right along with them. I knew what we were doing was wrong on so many levels, but he had to answer for his infidelity, not me. One time out of curiosity, I asked him did he feel any guilt about what he was doing. He responded by telling me not to concern myself with things that didn't concern me. Ever since that day, I learned not to meddle in his home life affairs.

During the embryo state of our relationship, Malik spoiled the hell out of me. He would send me flowers at work, and home just to tell me that I was on his mind. Poems and love letters arrived daily via mail, email, and text. Since we couldn't be together all the time, he would arrange monthly getaways as a form of escaping from our realities. These were the infamous company sponsored trips, I mentioned earlier.

Royalty was an understatement, when describing his mannerisms towards me during our times away. He would rub my feet, brush my hair, and even feed me strawberries while we drank champagne. We would fuck all night and sleep all day. In the mornings, he would run my shower, lay my clothes out on the bed and bathe me like I was a helpless infant incapable of taking care of myself. The list was endless with regards to all the things Malik did to make me fall in love with him, but reality is a cruel mistress. Now, a year later, I'm pregnant and I am sleeping not only with Malik, but I have a woman on the side, and baby daddy ain't got a clue.

****

"You okay baby?" Malik asked.

"Yeah, I'm fine, but let me ask you something." I sat up, looked straight into his eyes, and continued. "Do you love me Malik? I mean really love me?"

"Of course I do. What kind of question is that?"

"The kind that I need an honest answer to," I replied. "Have you ever thought about what would happen if I ever got pregnant?"

"Why, are you trying to tell me something Dee?" he asked with a hint of nervousness.

"No, it's just a hypothetical question."

Relieved he responded. "Danielle I don't know. I never thought about you getting pregnant. You already know my situation, and a kid-a kid would just complicate everything. Besides, why you even asking me what I'd do? The only obvious solution… you'd get an abortion."

There it was. He said it. I couldn't believe he said it. I had already known the answer to the question. I've even played it over and over again in my own head, but to hear the words come out of his mouth, I nearly sobbed out loud. He doesn't want me to have his kid. He doesn't want to be apart of my life like that. I am just something to do in between his marriage, whenever it was convenient for him. We would never be a family. The truth was finally settling in.

Malik obviously disturbed about what I had just asked him, walked towards the window, rubbing his chin as if he was in deep thought. Breaking his concentration, "Malik, I know what we agreed on. I didn't need a reminder," I snapped. "But shit happens sometimes you know," I said this as I walked towards the kitchen.

"You're on the pill aren't you?"

"No, Malik, I'm not. That's why we use condoms."

"We don't use them all the time Dee." I could hear the irritation and anger rising in his voice. "Are you trying to get pregnant?"

"Hell no," I yelled!

"Good, let's keep it they way. No need to fuck up a good thing right?"

"Right," I mumbled. "Wouldn't want to fuck up your good thing at home," I said as I excused myself to my bedroom. Still trying to maintain my composure, I fought to hold back the tears. I couldn't let him see me cry.

My pregnancy could not be found out. He made that perfectly clear. From the way he reacted, I thought for sure he was going to knock my ass out at the mere thought of me being pregnant. I guess I'll never be good enough, since I wasn't Angela. How could I have allowed this to happen? Malik doesn't want a life with me on that level. Why was I being so stupid? Why couldn't I be woman enough to let this man go? I questioned. Because I was weak for him, and that's why, I answered myself.

From my bedroom I could hear Malik out in the living room watching TV. He hadn't even come to check on me since I left the living room an hour ago, so I went out there where he was. Shit I was hurt and he needed to make me feel better. "You could've come and checked on me, to make sure I was okay." I said, pouring myself a glass of water. No answer. That son of a bitch acted like he didn't even here me. "You heard me Malik?" I yelled throwing a pillow at him.

"Yeah baby, damn, I heard you. You feeling better," he asked.

"As good as I'm going to feel I guess." Needing some type of affection, I sat down next to him and laid my head on his shoulder.

"You know I love you Danielle. You do know that right?"

"Sometimes I know and other times I'm not too sure Malik."

"Come here baby. Let daddy show you just how much." Clueless, it's just like a man to resort to sex as a means of fixing all female problems, but unfortunately, I wasn't interested.

In an attempt to make me feel loved, he got down on his knees in front of me and lifted my skirt. Knowing that I never wore panties unless my period was on, he knew he had easy access to my pussy. He licked me from top to bottom, moving his fat wet tongue in slow circular motions over my clit, causing my legs to shake involuntarily. Yeah, this was a real treat, because Malik didn't eat pussy too often.

I can't lie that shit started to feel real good, and my body began to yearn for his stiff manhood. At that moment, the only thing I could focus on was how wet and swollen my pussy had become. With fully raised nipples, I wanted nothing more than to take him into my mouth. Then suddenly, in the midst of it all, I became nauseous. Not wanting to alarm him, I fought the pressuring urge to regurgitate. But while I attempted to perform as usual, I was unable to fully disguise my illness, Malik noticed a difference.

Silent words of discontent spoke through his facial expressions, as he looked confused, and concerned all at the same time. Pretending to not notice a difference in my own actions, I sighed and moaned, as if I was being pleasured. Oh please…oh please, let him be done soon, I pleaded silently within myself. I didn't know how much more I was going be able to tolerate. The motion of him going in and out turned what was once pleasure just moments ago, into utter disgust presently. Coaching and encouraging myself to the very end, I managed to sustain, and my secret remained just that…my secret.

Chapter Thirteen

Bright and early the next day, Maxine arrived at my condo, propositioning the pregnancy test that she conveniently had stuffed in her purse. "So, do you want the test or not?"

"No, thank you. After you left last night I went to Walgreens and brought one myself, it tested negative, so please stop bugging me." I lied. I just wasn't ready to share that bit of information with anyone yet, primarily her. Like I suggested earlier, although I loved her to death, she had a big ass mouth.

"Whew, thank goodness," she said. "I would have been forced to hang out with Kevin and all his fairies alone if your ass was pregnant," she said laughing.

Kevin, the ultimate fairy had been one of our closest friends since high school. Maxine and Kevin hung out more, because they had more in common back then. They both were wild and would go to all the gay spots together. Max prowled for women. Kevin prowled for men. Together they were unstoppable. When Maxine told Kevin I was gay/bisexual, in honor of my newly found orientation he threw me a huge coming out party. I swear every queer in Miami was in attendance.

As flamboyant as he was, he was also renowned for his extravagant parties. One particular attribute associated with his parties was each one had its own theme. Every RSVP had to devote his or her full participation. Any attire less than fierce was neither acceptable nor admitted. This was an easy rule to live by for those who knew Kevin; they knew his protocol very well. Since no one ever really knew who was going to be in attendance, it was always a good idea to "dress to impress." Kevin liked to keep his attendees guessing; he believed it to be a motivating tool.

Speaking of parties, I had completely forgotten about Kevin's annual lingerie party this weekend. So much had been going on, that my mind had escaped me. I needed to get a new gown; something extremely tasteless and provocative. Being that I was blessed with these amazing pair of legs, and voluptuous breast, who was I to deny the world a sneak peak? Hell, pregnant or not, I was going to be Danielle Cyrus no matter what.

As an afterthought, I asked Max what she was wearing to the party. She didn't have a clue herself, so we decided to go shopping Friday after work. Out of the norm, Maxine stayed with me until I was dressed and ready for work. "You must not have any clients today?" I asked her as I locked my door and headed toward the elevator.

"No, not until this afternoon, besides, even if I did, my clients love me so much their willing to wait all day." She smiled.

"Conceited bitch," I joked, as we got into the elevator. She just smiled.

Most times, I had wished I followed in my girls footsteps and opened my own business. I dreamt of being a proprietor of my own establishment back in college, but Maxine was always the go-getter. I knew she would do it way before me. And she did. She owned a well-known salon in the heart of Liberty City. Yeah, it was mad ghetto, but the business was booming. Her regular clients visited the salon faithfully bi-weekly. Loyal they were. So loyal, that it didn't matter to them whether or not their rent was paid, their kids were fed, or their lights were in jeopardy of being cut off. Their physical appearance was their number one priority. A few things guaranteed of a ghetto girl: she would always get her hair, nails, and feet done. No matter what the sacrifice; sad but true.

Outside, by my car, we confirmed our visit to Fredrick's of Hollywood on Friday evening. Then we kissed and said good-bye. Soon after that, I was off to work, but not before I prayed to God asking for endurance, as I carried out my workday once more. I know it doesn't seem like it, but I loved what I did for a living. I just didn't particular like the people I did it with, which made a daily prayer a necessity.

In my car, I checked the messages on my cell phone, while sitting in the morning traffic. There was one from Kevin, reminding me of his party and the importance of being fierce. One was from my sweetie Lexy, wishing me a good morning, and one from Maxine last night, asking me about that damn pregnancy test; saying that I needed to swear off men, completely. Surprisingly, there was no message from Malik. That had been the first time since we've been dating that he hadn't called me, so I did what every woman would do…I called his ass! Hmm…I was greeted by his voicemail.

All that day, I stared at my phone waiting for him to return my call, but to no avail. My initial concern soon turned into anger, then my anger, slowly crept up to jealousy. When I left work, I called Malik again, and this time he answered.

"Damn, I've been calling you all day. What's up with you not answering your phone, or calling me?" I yelled!

"Lower your voice Danielle. I can hear you just fine without the yelling. I'm at the hospital with Angela."

"Oh…is everything ok?" I asked, as if I really cared.

"Well, it seems that she's having a miscarriage. Neither of us even knew she was pregnant. Ironic isn't it? You and I were just talking about pregnancy the other day, but she's OK considering her current circumstances. I'm sorry I didn't call you, but I will definitely call you later. I have to get back now. She's calling for me. I love you boo; we'll talk later."And just like that he was gone.

"Pregnant." I bet if she wasn't miscarrying right now, he would have gladly welcomed their new baby with open arms. But the idea of me being pregnant was unconceivable. *"Bastard!"*

Pissed off to the highest point of pisstivity-if that's even a word, I got home, put on my Kelly Price CD, and placed a wine glass in the freezer, so it would be nicely frosted by the time I got out of the shower. I needed to calm down and fast; alcohol has always worked for me whenever sex was not an option. I was far from an alcoholic, but when I couldn't fuck my problems away, I turned to my dear friends Mr. Seagram's Gin or Mrs. White Merlot.

Hot water and soap ran down my body as I harshly scrubbed in an attempt to wash away the stench of jealously that I had developed for Angela. I didn't want to permanently walk in her shoes; I just wanted to frequent them every now and again. Her life on the surface seemed so organized and so perfect. That for just one night, for one fraction of a moment, I wanted to know what it was like to sleep and awake with the same person everyday. To know that for better or for worse someone vowed to love me. Then I snapped out of it. Reminding myself that the same person she shares all that with, also shares himself with me, so what's the point of marriage? *Hmm...*

After my shower, I put on my terry cloth house robe, grabbed my wine glass out of the freezer and poured me a full glass. With nothing to watch on TV, I surfed through the channels for something interesting or comical to cheer me up. I could've really used a good laugh to help ease my mind. Thirty minutes of flipping through channels and nothing, so I decided to call Lexy to see if she was free and wanted to catch a movie or dinner.

"Hey sweetness," Lexy answered. "I was just thinking about you."

"Yeah, then why didn't you call me?" I joked.

"I just got home from work and wanted to freshen up first."

"Freshen up for what?" I asked her.

"Well, I was wondering if my girlfriend wasn't busy, that maybe she'd accompany me to dinner. I mean only if she wasn't busy of course," she teased.

"Don't play with me; you know I'd love to be your date tonight. I'll be ready in an hour."

"Okay, see you in an hour beautiful."

We hung up and I raced to my closet for something nice and enchanting to wear. It had been three days since I had last seen her, and I wanted to look extra special.

Literally, I tore my closest apart looking for the perfect outfit; something that wouldn't make me feel or look fat. I don't know if it was all in my head, but ever since I found out about being pregnant, I'd been feeling obese. Nothing seemed to fit the way it once did. After trying on pants, after pants, and skirt, after skirt, I finally settled on a short sassy, but classy, linen summer dress. At first sight, Lexy would know she had easy access to my goodies. She knew just as well as Malik, that I never wore panties unless it was that time of the month. And since it wasn't, I complemented the dress with matching heels and other accessories.

It was around 9:00 P.M. sharp when Lexy arrived at my home. She was always so punctual. I admired her for that. Me, on the other hand, I worked on CP time. If I told you I'd be ready at 7:00 P.M. that could easily turn into 8:30 P.M. I didn't do it on purpose, but it just always seemed to work out that way. Lexy had learned the hard way to always allow me at least an hour of preparation time, two in some cases.

Downstairs in the car, she passed me a bouquet of long stem yellow roses with a card that read: You complete me: Forever love, Alexis. Swept away by how caring she was, I leaned in and gave my baby a big wet thank you kiss. Lexy really loved me and that was easily measured just by the way she looked at me. I badly wanted to care for her on that same level, but I was too busy being Malik's personal jackass.

The hostess at the Cheesecake Factory advised us of the 30 minute wait time for a table, which was average for this time of the evening. Lexy and I sat at the bar, had a drink, and waited patiently in hopes of being seated sooner than 30 minutes.

The obvious distance between us was palpable. Lexy asked me what was on my mind. Unable to tell her the truth,

I lied and told her that I was thinking about a very important campaign I was working on for work. "Relax honey; think about work when you're actually at work. We're here trying to unwind and enjoy each other's company. Right now, I should be the only thing on your mind. OK?" she kissed my cheek, "I love you Ms. Cyrus; please relax for me."

She was right. I should have been focusing on her, but instead I was thinking about Malik's no good ass. Why was I thinking about someone who wasn't thinking about me? He was busy with his family, and I was left with my thoughts. No longer wanting to be a victim of circumstance, I knew the best thing to do once I got the abortion was to leave him alone.

Abortion... I couldn't believe that my life had resulted to this. I had read about abortions in books and I've spoken to women who had abortions before, but never once did I think it would ever be me. I really hated Malik for this. I thought he actually loved me. Although we agreed to never get pregnant, I always thought that if I ever did he would be happy. Guess the joke was on me. Obviously, Malik's love came with certain clauses—specifically, if you weren't Mrs. Malik Michaels.

"Roberts, table for two," the hostess called out over the microphone. Our table was finally ready, and I was famished. Me being a glutton for all the wrong type of foods, I ordered filet mignon, shrimp scampi, and a loaded baked potato; whereas, Lexy being a health freak ordered some type of grilled chicken and steamed vegetable platter. Her living habits were admirable. I, on the other hand…if it was full of fat, greasy, and covered in sauce, it was on my plate.

"You really should eat more vegetables, Danielle," Lexy commented as she took a bite of her steamed multi-vegetable medley.

"Don't start with me Lexy. You eat how you want without my input, so please don't lecture me on how I eat. My mother died along time ago and I don't think she was reincarnated as you."

I knew I was wrong for snapping at her, but she always had something to say about my eating habits, and I guess I was fed up with her comments and requests. I was already pissed off with Malik, so it didn't take much to take me over the top. But she didn't deserve that. "I'm sorry baby," I apologized, as I leaned in and gave her a kiss. "I've just got a lot on my mind and I took it out on you. I'm so sorry. You're right, you need to be the target of my concentration and for the remainder of the night I'm all yours."

After dinner we went for a walk on the beach figuring it would be nice to just take in the serenity of the ocean, while releasing all the stresses of the world. Holding her hand, I took in a deep breath and exhaled all my negative energy into the night's cool breeze. It had been a long time since we've just walked and talked. I enjoyed talking with her because she listened attentively without judgment. Lexy was so supportive of me, yet I couldn't understand why loving her the way she deserved to be loved was so hard for me to do. She was damn near perfect. Any woman or man would have been lucky to have someone like her in their lives. But here I stood, too stupid to realize the good thing starring me right in the face.

Minutes into our walk, we found a seat with a beautiful view of the ocean and sat down. Silence became us, and the ocean transformed into my sanctuary. My thoughts began to consume me again, as I thought about the past year with Malik and the past few months with Lexy. I thought back to the overnight weekend rendezvous I had with him, and how deceitful we had been towards his wife and kid. I also came into terms with how I knowingly accepted being second best to someone else, a thing I swore I would never do. With so many different recollections and emotions, I began to feel ill. Who had I become? What life could I possibly give a kid? I confirmed once again, there was no way I was going to have this kid who was conceived and based on lies.

With my last and final thought for the night, I turned to Lexy with tears in my eyes and said, "Baby, I apologize for all the things I should have done, and all the things I should not have done, to you, and for you. I have not been the woman you needed me to be, because of my own selfishness. But tonight I'm a changed woman. I do realize the jewel that sits before me. Lexy, I'm far from perfect, and mistakes will be made along the way, but rest assured a change is coming. You deserve the best." Then I sealed my affirmation with a kiss to her lips.

Shocked by my admission, and submission, she sat stiff, not knowing exactly what to make of what just happened. I knew she wanted to know where all that had come from, but uncertain of the answer, she refrained from asking. A single teardrop trickled from her eyes and down her rosy cheeks. Not tears of sadness, but tears of relief. Pleased with my confessions, she smiled the biggest and brightest smile I'd ever seen. I knew she had felt deprived in the past, so tonight was long overdue. I believe she, too, exhaled for the first time that night on the beach.

No more words were exchanged. There was nothing that needed to be added, or taken away from what was already said. Content with the nights ending, we sat nestled close together; arm in arm, in perfect tranquility. And I pledged to myself, that Lexy was no longer a convenience, but my number one priority for now on. *Fuck Malik!*

Chapter Fourteen

"Friday at last!" I shouted, as my alarm went off. I took a quick shower and was off to work. It was the launch of the weekend, so the traffic didn't bother me, nor did I get road rage. I was feeling great! It was pay day, and Max and I were going shopping in preparation for Kevin's party the following night. Being the Diva that I was, it was only natural that I scheduled a day of beauty for myself. Somebody had to show those queens how good they'd never look, no matter how much surgery they got, or make up they wore.

And of course, I couldn't forget about the women. The less attractive ones had to be green with envy, while the sexy ones filled with lust. Not that I would be interested in any of them, but I loved, and lived for the attention. Kevin would try, like he always did to outdo me. But like I told him all the time, he didn't stand a chance against natural, God made beauty. He hated whenever I told him that, but the truth was the truth.

I called Lexy from work just to let her know she was on my mind. Then I checked my messages to see if Malik had left one, since I had been ignoring his phone calls. Three messages waiting: One was from Maxine reminding me of shopping after work today, and the rest were from Malik:"Danielle, I'm sorry about the other night. I didn't mean to put you off; it's just that Angela was going through a rough time. Baby, I miss you. I miss your sweet voice. Call me when you get this message. I love you." That was the first message from his psychotic ass.

The second one sounded more agitated: "Damn Danielle, stop being so stubborn. You know you miss big daddy and big daddy misses you, too. I said I was sorry. Answer the phone!" Doesn't feel good Mr. Michaels does it? I said smiling to myself. I'll call his ass when I got good and ready to. Malik was the type of arrogant prick who thought the sun rose and fell with his ass, but he was about to have a rude awakening. There was no real urgency to return any of his calls right away, so I didn't. The thought of giving him a dose of his own medicine did my heart justice; time to see how he handled not being in control.

Tonight, was going to be all about me and Max. Personally, I believed that shopping was an antidote that healed all negative and stressful matters of the world. And I was in need of some serious healing. Anxious to start my weekend, I couldn't wait for five o' clock to come, but looking up at the clock on my wall; it was only ten minutes past twelve. Damn!

At 4:45 P.M. exactly, I began packing up my office, because at 5:00 P.M. sharp, I planned to be turning the ignition to my car. Today had been very trying for me. The company almost lost a multi-million-dollar contract due to a bullshit-ass campaign that a colleague of mine had

proposed during a staff meeting with some clients.
Apologetically, I had to intervene on the company's behalf,
and ask the clients to allow me 72 hours for a complete
campaign turnaround. I had to personally ensure the
success of their product through a newly revised proposal.
That situation alone made me want to break open the new
bottle of Patron that I had stashed away in my cabinet at
home…*TGIF!*

By 5:01P.M., I was already in my car screeching out
of the parking garage. I didn't hesitate when it came to
getting the hell out of that whole corporate bullshit
environment, primarily on a Friday. I called Maxine as soon
as I pulled out into traffic. She told me that she was on her
way to the mall and wanted to meet up in the food court.
After I hung up with her, reluctantly I called Malik.

"Why haven't you returned any of my damn calls?"
He immediately attacked me.

"Is this what I called you for? Do you need me to call
you back when you calm down?" I said nonchalant like.

"No…no, I'm sorry baby," he humbled himself. "I
just miss you. When can I see you?"

Sounding very uninterested, "Well tonight I'm
going to be busy, but let me get back to you about that OK?"
The tone in his voice relayed to me that he was not pleased,
but he was smart enough to know that he needed to stop
while he was ahead. Shit, he was already skating on thin ice,

it wouldn't have taken much for that bitch to crack and him fall right in.

As I hung up the phone, I spotted Maxine's truck parked on the first level of the over-sized parking garage. She owned a champagne colored, 2008 Avalanche with platinum rims. It rode real smooth. The love she had for her truck was no secret and for the money she spent on it, she better. Unlike her, I wasn't balling out of control with the Benjamin's. Yes, I was financially sound; therefore, I owned a simpler means of transportation; a black, 2009 Nissan Maxima, with the original manufactured alloy rims. It wasn't an Avalanche, but it was paid for.

Parked, Max spotted me walking in her direction and immediately started smiling. She was so juvenile at times. "Hey girl," she said as we embraced one another.

"Hey," I replied. Commencing to gossiping, as we as women so often did, I filled her in on Malik's current disposition with me and told her all about the messages he had left me, and how upset he was with me for putting him last on my priority list. She was pleased with how I handled myself, and insisted that I deal with him in that same manner from that day forward. Leaving my problems at the mall's entrance door, we walked inside and immediately there was a release of pressure from my burdened shoulders. Long over due, it was time for some TLC through shopping.

Fredrick's of Hollywood was unusually packed. Most of the people there seemed to be invited guest of Kevin's. There was an influx of lesbians, bisexuals, gays, and transgenders throughout the entire store. It looked like a damn circus. After an hour of evasive maneuvering through the crowd, I spotted a sexy black and gold gown with matching robe. It was sheer and came with a pair of matching laced g-string panties. The split in the front of the gown reached high up my thigh, leaving absolutely no room for imagination…it was perfect! With a quickened motion, I grabbed the gown from the rack before the other vultures had a chance to see it.

By the time I reached the check out counter, Maxine was already in line waiting to make her purchase. Slowly, I walked up behind her, clearly out of her peripheral view, and gently squeezed her butt. Her mannish ass didn't even budge an inch, as I violated her personal space. "Slut, you just let any body touch your ass? Nasty." I joked.

"We're in a lingerie shop, filled with lesbians on either side of us, do you really think I'd have a problem with anyone touching, squeezing, or even biting me on the ass right now?" We both laughed at the thought, as we waited in what seemed like the eight-mile line to checkout.

Content with my purchase, I asked Max if she wanted to grab something to eat. She agreed and we headed in the direction of the spacious food court. By the time we reached it, my stomach was touching my back, in other words, I was starving. Clutching tightly to her bag, as if someone was going to rob her, Maxine ordered her meal. I knew what was up with her. She didn't want me to see her outfit out of fear of me sweating her style. To be best friends, she was and always has been very competitive when it came to me. Guess that's just one of those catty traits that we as women all possess.

We left the mall, around 8:30. I was so tired from working all morning, then dealing with the crowd at Fredrick's of Hollywood. I just wanted to go home, take a long shower, and lay down. Next to her truck, Max and I said our good byes out in the parking lot of the mall; I thanked her for shopping with me, and told her I'd call her later, which in this case meant I'd call her tomorrow.

On the drive home, I checked in with Lexy to see what was on her agenda for the remainder of the night. I missed her. "Hey baby what are you doing?" I asked her.

"Nothing really, just sitting here thinking about you. What are you doing?"

"Actually, I'm leaving the mall with Max, on my way home now. I would love to see you, if that's possible."

"Yeah, of course; I was going to come see you tonight anyway."

"Oh, really?"

"Yeah, give me an hour. Have you eaten yet? If not, I'll pick up some dinner on the way there."

"No hun, I'm fine. All I need is you, I ate already."

"Okay, see you in an hour." We hung up.

When she arrived I was getting out of the shower. Lexy looked so sexy in her tight black jeans and t-shirt. Don't know if it was because I had been horny the last couple of days or what, but my plan was to get some of that tonight. In the kitchen she called out to me, "I'm about to fix me a drink, you want one?"

"Of course, I do honey. You know the rule of the house, no one drinks alone," I laughed. Tired from today's events, I contemplated going to sleep as I stared at the pillows on my bed while putting on lotion.

OK, so I did fall asleep. I hadn't planned on turning in so early, but once I laid my head down for a quick five minute nap, the rest was history. Surprisingly, Lexy wasn't upset about it at all. She just let me lie there peacefully. I felt her cover up me with the comforter on my bed, as she snuggled close against me. I reached for her arm and wrapped it around me, putting her to sleep as well.

The next morning, the delightful smell of bacon cooking and coffee brewing awakened me. I could not believe I had slept the whole night away. I went into the kitchen and there she was, my angel, with her sexy-ass. Body fully extended, she reached for a coffee mug; her Betty Boop t-shirt slowly rose with every attempt, slightly exposing her rosy butt cheeks from underneath. I smiled with delight. "Good morning sweet thang," I teased.

"Ah, baby, I wanted to serve you breakfast in bed. Please go get back in bed, so I can serve you." Without hesitation, I ran and jumped back in bed like a toddler high off sugar. Pulling the comforter up to my eyes, acting as if I never awoke, I waited for her to serve me breakfast in bed.

Minutes later she walked in the room carrying a tray filled with all my favorites: bacon, eggs, grits, biscuits, hash browns, jelly, butter, milk, orange juice, coffee, and a little vase with a single rose in it. Sitting it in front of me, she passed me a hand written note that read: *Here's to the first of many mornings. Forever love, Lexy.* This was the first time we ever really spent the whole night together since we've been dating, I thought to myself. Wow, now that the rose colored glasses were off, I could really see how much of my life Malik truly dictated. Because of him, I put limits on what I did or didn't do with Lexy and Ariel for that matter. Boy was I a fool, I'm just grateful she's still here after all my bullshit. Waking up to her was really nice; I could now see what I'd been missing.

"Thanks for breakfast babe," I said, taking a bit of my bacon.

As I washed my face and brushed my teeth in the bathroom, Lexy entered. The look on her face indicated to me that she was about to say something that I really didn't want to hear. "I'm so sorry, but I will be leaving soon. The hospital paged while I was cleaning the kitchen."

Disappointed, but empathetic towards her situation, "Don't apologize sweetie work comes first."

Before I could finish my last words, Lexy had positioned herself directly in front of me. "Danielle, nothing, or no one is more important than you. You mean the world to me, and if my world with you isn't OK, then nothing is. Do you understand that?" Starring at me, I knew she was sincere.

She wanted to cry. I could see the tears welling up in the corners of her eyes. I had to admit, I was touched; although, I didn't get why she was about to cry. "Yes, baby I understand," I assured her. Stepping closer together, simultaneously, we leaned in and passionately kissed, as if it were our very first time. Trying to keep in mind that she had to go to work, I denied myself of my wants, which was her in the bed with her legs spread wide open.

Apparently, work became the furthest thing from her mind. Leading me to the bed, she gently pulled the sheets back; far enough to allow her room to crawl into my space. She was half naked already, so there wasn't much left for me to do to get her to where I wanted her. Kissing and sucking my lips softly, she laid me down on the bed. The touch of her bare nipples against my skin was an instant turn on. Whispering softly, as she caressed my neck and fondled my ear lobe, "I know how much you love tasting me, but this is one sided today. All I want you to think about is how wet my pussies is, and imagine that you're indulging in every drop of it…" In pursuit of her own happiness, she proceeded down south, and her words played over and over again like a broken record; echoing in my ear.

Lexy skillfully at play, slowly grazed her plump lips across my bulging clit, while moaning out of her own arousal. Painfully engorged, my pussy was pounding hard begging for an instant relief.

"Oh, baby don't tease me, she's already purring for you," I said, as I let out a whimpering sound.

"Oh really, well I guess I need to pet my pussy, so she'll calm down huh? This is my pussy isn't it?"

"Yes, baby-yes. This is your pussy," I surrendered, as she ate me out in a way that had to be illegal in some country, somewhere.

Hearing how vocal she became as put me in the mind set of someone doing her, at the same time she did me. That thought heightened my urge to come ten times over. I didn't want to cum yet; then again I did. My body took control over my indecisiveness; I began to grind my hips forcefully in a circular motion. Grabbing hold of Lexy's hair, I thrust my cunt into her face. "Baby I'm about to cum," I chanted.

"Me too, Ooh…baby, me too!" The two of us climaxing at the same time had never happen before. Visualizing her face while enjoying the vibrations of her body as she came, made me cum harder and longer than I ever came in my life.

My body shook and my legs quivered as I came down off my high. Lexy at eye level now, kissed my forehead then my lips. The remnant of my exploding vagina was smeared, glossed all over her mouth. "Eww, you got cum all over your face," I joked.

"Yeah, and it tastes good too," tracing her tongue along the outline of her mouth.

"You're nasty Lexy."

"And you love me for it." She was right; I loved how freaky she was in the bedroom. On the outer surface you wouldn't expect her to have one nasty bone in her body, but this girl was a lady in the streets and a freak in the sheets.

Lexy went into the bathroom to prepare for work as I lay in bed still reeking of sex; I turned over on my stomach with my ass still exposed. I started thinking about Lexy's mental status. Lately, she'd been more emotional and clingy. Her behavior had begun to alarm me. Like how she acted in the bathroom, when I told her I understood work came first, her reaction was strange, because my comment didn't warrant her intense response. And the tears, what was that about? Anyway, brushing her odd behavior to the side, I did what everyone did after a good nut…Yes; I took a much-needed nap, while she got dressed for work.

It was late in the afternoon when I finally woke up. Good food and great sex; can't beat that with a stick. My day was going to be all off track. I still had to get my hair done, my nails done, a wax, and a pedicure, before Kevin's party.

How was I going manage to get all that done in a matter of four hours? Lord, I needed a miracle and I needed it fast.

Picking up the phone, I called Max to see what she was doing. To my surprise she had also just awakened.

"Hey girl, what you doing?" I asked her in between yawns.

"Apparently the same thing you were doing." We both chuckled.

"Look I am running way behind, and I have so much to do before tonight. I need your help." I said desperately.

"Sure babe. Anything you need."

"Great. First I need you to do my hair, and then get your best manicurist to do my feet and nails, while I sit under the dryer. Also, please call to schedule me a wax with that French guy you go to all the time, and tell him I want the works." Spitting my demands out like I was placing a to-go order in the drive thru of McDonald's, Max interjected,

"Damn. Anything else Queen Sheba?"

Checking myself, "Sorry, didn't meant to handle you like that; I just want to be nice for tonight. You know we have to represent especially, since Kevin and his friends try to out do the natural, genetically correct women. I'm just out to show them they can't fuck with Mother Nature." We both laughed girlish laughs, and continued our conversation about Kevin and his friends for at least 10 minutes before hanging up.

I had no real animosity towards Kevin and his friends; it was just a rivalry that we have been keeping up for the last 10 years. He was one of my dearest friends, but just as catty as me and Max. Always trying to have one up on us, saying that anything we can do, he can do it better. And on some occasions he really did. Kevin spent many hours and dollars to look as glamorous as he did, and I didn't blame him at all for being so competitive.

I remember when he first started to transition, he was nervous and excited all at the same time. Max and I were his biggest supporters; we attended every doctor's consult, pre-op, and surgery. Kevin's parents had turned their back on him way back when we were in college, so without the support of his biological family, we were thrilled to have been there for him.

****

His secret was found out the first year he was away from home. While cleaning his room, his mom stumbled upon his journal, which detailed all the explicit sexual encounters and thoughts he had of men/boys, going as far back as grade school. Rushing to pack, he had mistakenly left it behind after he moved out to live on campus.

That following Christmas was the first and last time Kevin saw or heard from any of his family members, and that had been well over nine years ago. Upset, volatile, and filled with rage, Kevin's father threw the carving knife onto the dinning room table and stormed out in the middle of dinner. At the time, no one but his wife knew what was bothering him. Heedless to the fact that his father knew his secret, Kevin chased after him, finally finding him on the front porch.

"Dad, are you OK?" Ignoring his son's efforts to communicate with him, he kept his gaze to the woods that surrounded their family home. Stepping in closer, Kevin repeated, "Dad, are you OK?" Placing his hand on his dad's shoulder, he father jolted out of his dead man's stare.

"Don't fucking touch me queer!"

"Excuse me," Kevin said, confused and offended by his father's chosen words.

"All this time, all these years, and you knew…Why? What did we do so wrong that you had to look to men for sexual comfort?

Eyes wide open and unable to justify his sexual preference, Kevin stood frozen as his father spoke, revealing his darkest shame to all who listened. Demeaning him as a man, and as his son, his father continued, "Men are supposed to be with women, not each other. How could you? No, I won't accept this in my house or in my family." He asserted. "If you continue to live in this manner, you are no longer apart of this family. I will not condone this-this-so called life style of yours; my son is not gay. I'll see you dead, before I accept you as a faggot."

Faggot. The most hurtful reference in regards to a gay man, and this was how his own flesh and blood saw him. Kevin's heart shattered into a million pieces. Even his mother stood speechless, as she observed their conversation from behind the screened front door. She didn't try to intervene as her husband verbally abused her only son, nor did she console him, or offer him any words of encouragement after his father was done. In her old-fashioned way, she adopted her husband's beliefs and decisions as her own. Witnessing her son's agony, cowardly, all she could do was lower her head to keep from looking at him.

Hurt beyond repair, Kevin tried to explain to his father that he didn't choose to be gay, and he did not want to be banished from the family. His father, a God fearing man, head strong believer of the bible teachings of homosexuality, disregarded his son's plea for forgiveness and acceptance; instead, he instructed Kevin to gather the rest of his belongings, minus his journal, which his father previously burned, and told him to leave the home from which he was raised, and warned him to never return.

Slamming the screen door behind him, Kevin's father went back into the house, and his mother followed; leaving the rest of us on the porch astounded.

Down on his knees on the cold wooden porch, Kevin sobbed loudly. Max and I were infuriated at how brutal his father spoke to him. We cried as we knelt down next to him and held each other for what seemed like an eternity. While embracing him like that, Max realized how blessed she was that her family openly accepted her as she was. We all vowed from that day forward to always be there for each other. With wobbling legs, he stood and walked away from his now estranged family forever.

But Kevin was not without a family. The three of us remained tighter than glue to this day. On holidays we would cook and celebrate together, just like a normal family of three. I knew Kevin thought of his family often, but he respected his father's wishes and because he accepted himself as a gay man, he never reached out to them again. That night on the porch when his father left him in the cold, Kevin the son died, and Kevin the queen was born shortly after.

****

It had been a trying journey for him, but finally he stopped mourning the death of Kevin the boy from seven years ago. He now rejoiced in the beautiful cosmetically constructed Kevin—transgendered woman. And with the love and support of not only Max and I, but his own circle of close knit friends, he had really grown into his own. He has made a very comfortable living for himself through the publication of his memoir, and he is abundantly loved by all who encounter him.

No longer burdened by shame, or rejection, he had finally realized that the only true path to his happiness was to let go of all negative influences. But above all things

Kevin had to learn to love Kevin—and he did. To this day, nobody loved Kevin more than Kevin loved himself.

Chapter Fifteen

The salon was packed as usual on a Saturday. I was just so afraid to enter Max's place of business sometimes due to how ghetto fabulous it was. But it was profitable and Max loved it. The revenue she made monthly from her grammatically challenged customers was considerably gratifying financially, and well worth the daily bullshit she had to deal with.

Inside there were women of all shapes, sizes, colors, and nationalities waiting to be served. One could have easily mistaken the salon as a sports bar by how loosely people used foul language. Thankfully, there weren't any kids being serviced at the moment. Not that it would have mattered to them, but it would've annoyed the hell out of me. Yeah, I know I got a mouth on me, but damn! I cringed at most of their conversations and wished that I could've washed a few of their mouths out with a bar of soap.

Looking around, the thing that really pissed me off was that some of the finest women in the world were straight from the ghetto; born and raised. Not just your typical pretty lady, but curvaceous, gorgeous women. They were beautiful on the outside, but utterly useless on the inside. Maybe with their mouths taped shut, I would've probably given a few of them the time of day. Because regardless of how straight a woman claimed she was, given the right person and circumstance, she could easily be turned out.

"Danielle... Hi, please come this way." A beautiful young woman interrupted my critical thinking of Maxine's patrons. She had to be in her early 20s, standing at about 5'5, and weighing about 145lbs. Her skin was smooth like creamy caramel and I got a whiff of her scent as a breeze whisked in through the ajar back door; the stylists always left the back door open to help with the ventilation system. And with heightened senses due to my pregnancy, I inhaled all those hazardous fumes associated with a salon as I walked to the back of the building where the shampoo stations were located.

"My name is Candace; Max just pulled into the driveway and asked me to get started on you for her. We'll start by shampooing and conditioning your hair. Do you know what style you want today?" Her voice was not raspy, and she spoke clearly unlike the other women who worked in the salon. I was blown away. Pleasantly captivated, I heard the sounds of her voice and I saw her lips part, but nothing she said came together to form complete sentences for me. Literally, I sat there deaf, dumb, and blind.

"Danielle," Max shouted.

"What?" I barely replied.

"Girl you didn't hear me calling you?"

"No I didn't. I was day dreaming or something."

"Well wake your ass up and think of the style you want, cause I don't have all day. I got to get ready for tonight too. Kimono, the nail chick, is going do your manicure and pedicure while you're under the dryer."

Kimono...wow how cliché, I thought to myself.

"Your wax appt is at six, so we must hurry. The party starts at eight, but since we're going to be fashionably late, we have until ten."

"OK...OK, grouchy lady. I'm thinking...I'm thinking. In the meanwhile, go do something with yourself."

"I am. I'm about to wash your hair to get you out of here. Thank you Candace, but I'll take it from here," Max said, as she leaned me back, positioning me for my wash.

"Uh, Max, I want her to wash my hair if you don't mind. I'm kinda enjoying her presence, if you know what I mean," I hinted to my friend. Knowing exactly what my request meant, she pinched my arm and called Candace back over.

"On second thought, you can finish her for me and I'll prepare a work station to style her hair." Walking away from me, Max mouthed the words, "Nasty heifer."

In return, I mouthed, "And you know this." Leaning back in the black adjustable chair, I anxiously waited for Ms. Candace to begin massaging my scalp, as well as my imagination.

Finally, I finished at the salon around 5:15, made it to my waxing appointment on time and was back at home around 7:20 P.M. Boy the things we as women endured for just a few hours of envy. My skin was on fire from top to bottom from where I was waxed. During the treatment I had to ask the technician if any skin came off with the hair, because that's what it felt like. Next time, I'll just take the time to shave at home. That way I'd save time and money, but most of all I'd avoid a whole lot of unnecessary pain.

It was around 7:45 P.M. when Max called to make sure I was getting dressed and drunk all at the same time. Like a good girl, I was. My Absolut Vodka and cranberry juice was right next to me. I gave myself one good look over before I finished getting dressed. "You sure are fine," I said to myself, as I sipped my drink and smiled.

My phone rang again, and right when I was about to pick it up something told me to look at the caller ID first. I'm glad I did. It was Malik. He got some nerve. He must've really thought that the sun rose and fell on his ass. Sorry Mr. Michaels, it's all about the ladies tonight. See how you like the back burner for a while. With one quick touch of the finger, I sent Malik's ass straight to my voice mail, which happened to feature Beyonce's song "Irreplaceable." I know that pissed him off, but oh well. As my father used to say, "It's better to be pissed off then pissed on."

It was 9:00 P.M. when Max arrived at my house. Luckily, she was my best friend in the whole wide world or I would have been trying to get at her. Very well put together, she looked absolutely gorgeous. Flawless make up, hair up in a genie style ponytail, and her leather one-piece was practically painted on, cupping all the right curves in all the right places. She was my best friend, so I'm not gonna finish telling all the things I was thinking about her at that moment. Simply put, she highly resembled Halle Berry, in the movie "Catwoman." Truth be told, I ain't had nothing up on Max tonight. And I would have gladly been the kitten to her litter if we weren't best girls.

"Danielle, what are you doing? If I didn't know better, I would be under the assumption that you were checking me out," she grinned.

"Whatever chick, you look alright," I said, as I turned my back to her while gathering my things so we could leave.

"Good! Then put your eyes back in your head and let's go."

"Whatever." That's all I could say, at least that's all I would allow to come out my mouth in the name of friendship.

As planned, we arrived to Kevin's house fashionably late as usual. Maxine preferred it that way. She loved to be the center of attention on any given occasion. Outside, along the street, there was barely anywhere to park, but we caught someone leaving as we pulled up. "Girl this party is so thick," I said to Max.

"Did you expect anything less?" We jumped out of the car, and I text Lexy goodnight as we walked up the sidewalk to the stylishly laid out extravaganza. To the naked eye one would've assumed that this was some kind of red carpet event with the exception of no real celebrities.

When we walked through the front door all eyes were on us just as we planned them to be. You could feel the acute stares of the envious and the lustful, and hear the poorly muffled sounds of whispers as we sashayed across the overly crowded room filled with our own kind. We were eating the attention up. The intensity throughout the room was unmistakable, but I didn't mind. We were getting the exact outcome we both had hoped for and with the gown I was wearing, I was sure to stir some things up.

"Ladies, glad you finally decided to grace us with your presence." Kevin sarcastically greeted us with a grin on his face.

"Well, better late then never. Besides, you can't rush beauty like this," I barked back.

"Touché," was Kevin's only reply, as he looked us both over one last time. "Still not as beautiful as I am," He said, walking away as if he was on the catwalk at a pageant. Maxine and I just laughed. He, along with the rest of the wannabe queens would never understand that what Mother Nature creates may be imitated, but never duplicated.

"I'm going to get a drink Danielle, do you want one?" Max asked.

"Of course, I haven't reached my limit yet." Focused, Max disappeared into the crowd. Kevin truly went all out for this bash as expected. The décor of the room was soft and romantic, keeping in the theme of lingerie party. Rose pedals met you at the door and were scattered in no particular order across the floor. For the freaks in attendance, there was a carpeted runner leading to the back rooms of Kevin's five bedroom - four bathroom house.

Candles were lit throughout, creating the perfect romantic setting. Some were on the mantel above the fireplace, while others were on the tables, and mounted on the walls down the hallway. Soft music played in the background, and in the middle of the living room floor stood an oversized heart shaped bed—in lieu of his normal living room furniture. The bed was hidden behind oversized sheer curtains, and from what I could see there was rose pedals sprawled out on the bed, along with experimental sexual paraphernalia. Lord only knew what Kevin had planned for the nights' entertainment.

Maxine returned and handed me my drink; that was pretty much the last time I saw her for the rest of the night, which was cool with me. I knew most of the people there and if I didn't, I was sure to know them by the end of the night. After about an hour of no supervision, I was nice and tipsy. Not drunk. A lady never gets sloppy drunk, just pleasantly tipsy; and that I was.

Trapped in my own little world, every song that played from the sound system became my favorite song. I didn't have a care in the world. Two stepping to Robin Thick's song, "Lost without you." Suddenly, what was undeniably the bulge of perfectly rounded breast were firmly pressed against my back. Now remember I mentioned earlier that I was pleasantly tipsy, then out of nowhere comes this woman, none-the-wiser of the trouble she was about to get herself into.

My heart raced as she gently slid her arm around my waist without saying a word. Presumptuous, she pulled me closer to her and we began to slow grind to the rest of the song. I was lost in her presence, but there was something oddly familiar about this woman. I knew her odor - not in a bad way, but I've smelled her before. Perfectly synchronized, our bodies danced as if being reunited. Her aura, I knew this woman in more ways than one. I won't lie, I was reluctant to turn around and face the stranger, but I had to-I just had to know.

Slowly, and cautiously, I turned to face her and my mouth hit the floor. I couldn't believe it; Ariel was standing directly in front of me. I knew I recognized the scent of her breath and the rhythm of her waist. Mesmerized, I couldn't stop staring!

"Close your mouth before something flies in it," she said, as she closed it for me.

"Ariel, what…I mean how-? I'm sorry I'm just so surprised. How are you?"

"I'm good Danielle, but I'm even better now that I've seen you. You look great," she said, as she checked me from head to toe.

"You look good too," I complimented.

"So who are you here with?" She asked with very little interest in my response.

"I'm here with my best friend Max. What about you?"

"I'm solo. A friend of mine knows Kevin and invited me, but I can't find him anywhere now. He's probably bent over somewhere," she laughed.

"Can I get you a drink?" she asked.

"No, thank you. I think I had enough."

Talking with Ariel again felt like old times. In an instant, I was taken back to the first time we informally met on *Blackplanet*. All the butterflies I once felt for her, were reborn and fluttering around in the pit of my stomach. She sipped from her drink as we caught up on past times in between dances. She was still the same sweetheart I met way back when. Ignorant to the time, we hadn't noticed how the room dramatically cleared out from the other guest leaving. We had no clue as to how late it had gotten.

Rebellious to the thought of leaving her, I decided I was going to ask her to leave the party with me. I hadn't realized just how much I've missed her, until now. I stood there talking and looking at her. It was funny how all the emotions I thought had escaped me for Ariel found their way back into my heart.

"If you don't have any plans for the remainder of the night, I would love to continue this conversation at my house," I spoke out of fear of never seeing her again.

"No, I don't, but do you think that would be a good idea with you still seeing Malik and all? I remember very well what you told me he said about that night, and I'm assuming that's the reason we no longer kick it right?"

"Yeah that's true, but that's also in the past. Things have changed since we last spoke. So the question remains, will you accompany me home tonight?"

"I would love to if you're sure its OK, but I don't remember how to get to your place."

"Just follow me. First I need to find Max to tell her I'm gone. Knowing her, she's sure to be in between someone's child's thighs as we speak."

And just as expected she was upstairs in Kevin's Jacuzzi with some Asian looking chick. She was nice and wasted too. I asked her if she was OK, and if she was ready to leave. She told me she was staying at Kevin's; he would bring her to get her car tomorrow. Knowing that she was in good hands, I kissed my friend good night and told her, "Don't do anything I would do." Laughing, I kissed her lips again, and then set off downstairs to get Ariel.

At the bottom of the stairs she waited patiently for me. She was just as beautiful as I remembered her to be. "Is Max OK?" she inquired.

"Yeah, she's in good hands. You ready?" Grabbing our coats from the closet, I briefly quizzed her to see if she remembered the type of car I drove. Reciting my vehicle to me, she was coherent and on point with the description. I left her to go get into my car and encouraged her to keep up.

Ariel proved to be an excellent trailer. Without skipping a beat, she followed me home. Luckily for me, she wasn't in the business of stalking people, at least I hoped.

Chapter Sixteen

Inside, I offered her something to drink and I had another myself. She looked amazing in her lingerie. Her stature was magnificent. She wore a gold, backless silk gown that embraced her every curve. From the way her gown clung to her body, I could see that she had no panties on underneath. When she moved, her camel's foot revealed itself, as the material traced along the outline of it. I had to break the direction of my concentration, to counteract the swelling between my legs. Sex was not why I invited her to my place and I didn't want to give her that impression. I really just wanted to talk to her some more, nothing more or less.

Sitting there in the wee hours of the morning with a friendly face compelled me to come clean for once. Ariel was no longer a part of the fucked up equation known as my life, so I knew her take on the matters would be bias free. I had a lot of shit on my chest and really needed to expel some of it.

I wasn't sure whether or not she would be open to hear all that burdened me, but I took a chance anyway, and began to spill all that had been loading me down for quite some time now. Liberating myself, I opened with my biggest secret of all, my pregnancy. She tilted her head sideways in confusion. Because I had been drinking heavily, she held her tongue and listened. I went on to tell her that she was the only one who knew about it and how I was considering abortion. My relationship with Lexy soon followed the plans of abortion. And lastly, I explained to her about why I ended my relationship with her so abruptly. I told her how much she had meant to me, and how I often wondered if there was ever a real chance at us again. Malik held all the cards back when she and I were involved, but I assured her that I was holding all my own cards now, kind of. I still hadn't officially broken it off with him yet, but that was definitely on the horizon.

Fucked up I know. With how crazy my world was with Malik and Lexy, why in the hell was I trying to rekindle anything with Ariel right? Well I don't know. She just felt right to me. After all, she was my first woman experience and you know what they say about your first. Judging by the questionable expression on her face, I started to wonder if I had made a mistake by having a confessional at four in the morning while intoxicated.

"Do you love Lexy?" she asked, staring directly in my eyes.

"I'm not sure. I do care a lot about her. I want to love her, but seeing you again makes me unsure of my feelings all over again."

"You must first be true to yourself Danielle. You have to figure out what you want, because I won't knowingly enter into a fucked up situation with you." I didn't like Ariel's response, but I had no choice, other than to respect it. I didn't push the issue with her. She was right. It was time I grew up and put my life in order.

Feeling very needy, I asked her if she would be so generous as to stay the night with me. Nothing sexual, I just needed to be held, and I wanted to be held by her and only her. She agreed. Turning off the lights, crawling into bed, she slid close behind me, spooning with me until we both drifted into a sound sleep.

Morning came and went. The blazing evening sun shone through the cracks of my wooden blinds, awaking Ariel and I around 5:30 P.M. Since it was so late in the evening we chose to go out for something to eat and catch a movie. Lucky for Ariel we wore the same size clothes. I told her to help herself to whatever she wanted to wear in my closet. Usually I was overly anal when it came to loaning my clothing to someone, but I appreciated her staying with me last night, so I expressed my gratitude through my selflessness.

Ariel, knowingly undressed in front of me, I'm only human, so yes, I watched intently as she disrobed piece by piece. Her body mold was just the way I remembered it to be. "Are you coming?" she asked. Before she could finish her sentence, I was already half naked. Stepping into the warm bubble filled tub, I sat between her legs with my back against her breast. Thrilled and comforted by her company, I laid my head back on her shoulder and kissed her cheek softly. Returning the favor, she leaned slightly forward and gave me an innocent peck to the side of my face.

I craved intimacy from Ariel, but I refrained from acting on it. Everything in me wanted to take her face, insert my tongue into her mouth, intentionally provoking the on set of foreplay. But I didn't know how she would react to me doing that, so going against my wants; I maintained the innocence of our time together and did nothing. Ariel on the other hand, knew me better than I thought. She knew I was holding back, so she leaned in and made the first move.

Outside the tub we dropped our towels as we kissed and walked towards the wall of the bathroom. Gently pushing me against the wall, she suckled at my neck, my ears, and my breast. My pussy was on fire for her. Ariel guided herself all over my body, reclaiming her territory. Surpassing my belly button, she fondled my clit with her middle finger. Going up and down, round and round, circles, circles…oh yes circles!

I barely kept my stance against the wall. She partially parted my legs, got down on her knees, and continued to entice me with a combination of licking and sucking on my clit. Receiving all of me into her mouth, cum ran down my leg without waste. Ariel made sure to confiscate every drop that escaped my inner lips. Her slippery tongue played inside my throbbing hole, as I hungrily begged for more. She then shoved two fingers inside, intensely fucking me.

First slow, then fast, all while keeping a steady concentration on my lady pearl.

"Ah, fuck," I screamed! "It feels so good baby, don't stop…don't stop…please…baby don't stop." Desperately, I tried to fight the arising orgasmic blast, which was surely developing between my legs, but I lost horribly. Grabbing Ariel by the head, I grinded ferociously atop her face; ultimately, reaching my peak. My legs shivered beneath me, as I reached for something to maintain my balance.

Sensually, smooching her way up the extension of my now fragile frame, reaching me at eye level, I embraced her full, round breast between my petite hands; teasing her nipples by applying adequate pressure with my index finger and thumb. Moaning, she insisted I squeeze harder. So I did. My mission was to re-discover every inch of her body, as I took her breast into my mouth. Loving it, she reached her hand up from her side and slid her fingers one by one into my mouth; forcing me to taste my own sweetness that had dried up on her fingers. *Mmm…*

"My turn," I flirted as I made my way down her midsection. I rubbed between her legs along side her cat, and slightly touched it just enough to make it purr; I was careful not to give her too much too soon. I wasn't ready for this to be over yet.

"Taste me baby…taste me," she begged. I ignored her plea. The more eager she became, the wetter she got. When I thought she had had enough and was ripe for the picking, I then buried my face in her pussy. Slow, steady strokes were how I twirled my tongue while I sampled every crevice of her and made sure all parts received their just deserts.

With my index and ring fingers, I massaged inside her vaginal walls, while nibbling at her engorgement. "Oh my God!" she screamed, clawing my back with her finger nails. "Oh baby, I'm cumming…I'm cumming!" And she did… all over my face. Nothing beats a good facial, I thought to myself, licking the remnants of Ariel from my upper lip.

Needless to say, after that session in the bathroom, we stayed in and ordered Chinese for dinner. I called May Fu, a Chinese restaurant down the street from where I lived. They were infamous for their egg rolls and honey chicken.

We placed an order for special fried rice -no vegetables, honey chicken chunks, two egg rolls and some fortune cookies. The order taker told me the total and advised me that it would take at least 30 minutes for delivery. That was just enough time to freshen up "for real" this time, and order a pay per view movie to watch.

I allowed Ariel to bathe first. We deemed it safer to shower alone versus together. When she got out, I handed her a sexy little red nightgown that had a high slit up the side, exposing (for my benefit) her sexy ass thighs. Stepping out of the shower, I heard the doorbell ring as I put my robe on. Damn, they got here fast, I said to myself. "Babe, get that for me please," I yelled from the bedroom. There was a dead silence in the living room, so I called out to Ariel, but got no answer.

Stepping from the bedroom into the living room, I saw Ariel standing at the door-frozen, mouth slightly ajar. "Babe, did you hear me calling you?" I asked walking up behind her. Pulling the door open wider, "How much do I...oh fuck," looking up from the money in my hand, only to find myself face to face with Malik.

Chapter Seventeen

"What the fuck! You're fucking gay now, Danielle?" Malik bellowed with rage. "Ariel, what the fuck is you doing here?" Apprehensive, she backed up. The look in her eyes was a clear indication that she was in a fight or flight state of mind. I couldn't blame her. Malik had death in his eyes. Her fear of him and the current situation, escaped through the stream of tears that fell down her face. She was frightful of what may have happened next, and so was I. I had never seen him so angry. I wasn't sure what Malik was capable of when pushed to the limit.

"Ariel, please go to the bedroom," I insisted. But before she could move, Malik had pushed me to the side and grabbed her by the arm. Shaking and shoving her through the front door, he threatened to kill her if he ever saw her near me again. Throwing her out the door like common trash, he gathered her belongings and tossed them out in the hall way with her. Before I could say or do anything, the door had slammed in Ariel's face.

My heart broke in so many pieces. Internally, I silently cried out to her for what he had done. I attempted to go after her, but Malik stood firmly placed in front of the door—barricading me inside my condo. The repulsion on his face dared me to challenge him.

"Danielle, what the hell is going on?" Unmoved to answer his question, I didn't. "Oh, you don't want to talk now huh? What the fuck is this all about? How long have you been sleeping with her behind my back? Answer me bitch!" he said, temporarily loosing his damn mind.

"Bitch, oh now I'm a bitch? You got some nerve. You think that you can just come and go in my life whenever it's convenient for you, and expect me to seat idly by while you sleep with me one night and your wife the next? While you take family trips and plan vacations," sobbing, I continued. "You expect me to play second best forever Malik, with no other outlet? No. Not any more. I have people. No, correction, I have women who care about me, and I about them.

"Women," He repeated with a puzzled look on his face.

"Yes, women," I confirmed.

Fed up with him all together, I was ready to let him in on all the bullshit that was presently going on in my life. "You may want to have a seat," I suggested to him. Unsure of my reasoning for him to take a seat, he obliged my request. "Malik, shit is real fucked up in my world right now, and since your apart of my chaos, it's time you knew the depths of my troubles."

Seated on the furthest end of the couch, he waited. Finding great comfort in his distance away from me, I took a deep breath and said a short prayer as I allowed my secrets to unveil one by one.

To start, I explained to him how my new found love for women resulted from that one night with Ariel, and the struggles I went through trying to deny what I was feeling for the same sex. I opened his eyes to the fact that I did break it off with Ariel, but found myself craving women. I told him about going to the gay club with Max and meeting Lexy there. Educated him on how much love and admiration she had developed for me during our short relationship. And believing that he needed to know all the ingredients of my involvement with Lexy, I shared all the specific details of our strong friendship, as well as our intimacies, so he could better understand the full bond between Lexy and I. He needed to know that it wasn't just sex between us.

Once I was done with speaking on past events, eventually I started to talk more about current events; leading up to how I became reunited with Ariel at Kevin's party. Checking his status, I lifted my head and made minimal eye contact with him, and there was nothing good within his eyes. Rubbing his head and scratching his chin, this worried me. I wasn't sure if I should continue, or tell him about the pregnancy. Judging by his already irritated disposition, being pregnant may have been the only thing that kept him from hitting me, so I continued.

"Malik I know you have taken in a lot tonight, but there's one more thing I need to tell you." Uneasy with being within his reaching distance, I walked to the back of the couch, near the cordless phone sitting on the end table. If he wanted me, he would have to put in the effort to get to me, by then, I would have already dialed 911.

Another deepened breath and another quick prayer to the Lord Almighty I blurted out, "I'm pregnant and it's yours."

Standing from his crouched position on the couch, and with a great look of disgust in his eyes, his chest rose and fell rapidly then he roared, "Pregnant! Bitch you pregnant? Guess that wasn't just a hypothetical question the other day huh? You-you set me up for failure. I told your ass that I wasn't interested in having any kids outside of my marriage and you fucking knew that. What did you think that I'd leave my family? Are you crazy? You must be." Grunting, Malik started towards me as if he was about to strike me, but hit the wall behind me instead.

Staring at the big unexplainable hole in my wall, I grew frantic. I didn't know what to expect. Clearly in flight mode, I ran towards the front door, and reached for the door handle, but Malik grabbed me by the arm saying, "Hoe, you ain't going nowhere," throwing me to the couch, "sit your ass down."

Hovering over me he said, "So let me ask you this, did you really think I was gonna leave Angela and my child

148

for you? Danielle I told you repeatedly that I have a family, whom I love very much, and if you think I'd abandon them for your confused dyking ass, you are sadly mistaken. Just because you suck a mean dick, doesn't make you wife material." He snarled his remarks.

His words cut through my soul like a hot knife through cold butter. Aspiring to stand firm and appear unmoved, I failed miserably. Salty tear drops fell from my flushed cheeks onto my robe, as I stood in complete disbelief of how he was talking to me. I couldn't believe it was only weeks ago that I lay in his arms with thoughts of forever, and now this. At present, the man that stood before me was unknown – a stranger.

Hysterically laughing like a crazed person, he continued, "oh yeah, you gon' get an abortion and if you don't do it, then I'll kill the son of a bitch myself." From the glossed over look in his eyes, I knew mentally he had clocked out, and he was dead serious about me getting an abortion. Matter of fact, I knew that ridding myself of this pregnancy was the only logical thing to do any way.

All the love I once had for him came to an immediate demise. The only emotion remaining was resentment. A prompt eradication of this pregnancy was top priority. The sooner I cleansed my body of his seed, the sooner I could cleanse my life of him.

Thinking back on all the sacrifices I've made during the time I've known him, infuriated me. How many numerous nights had I spent at home alone, while he was with his precious family? I had compromised my dignity and my self respect by accepting second best in his life. I had been a true glutton for punishment, because I knew Malik was bad for my health a long time ago. Ignoring what I knew to be morally wrong, I sat as a prisoner in my own home paying for my mistakes.

Ceasing his ranting long enough to catch his breath; "Here's five hundred dollars, this should cover the cost of the abortion." He threw the money at me like a cheap whore that he had just fucked. Emotionless, I sat there dissecting the massive hole in my in my heart. And as if he hadn't said enough, he felt obligated to add one last commentary, "Oh, by the way freak, your services are no longer needed nor desired, so don't bother calling me any more. And I expect you to do what's best for you by getting that abortion as soon as possible." Getting close to my face, "I swear if anyone finds out about this, I'll be back, and trust me you don't want me to come back." And just like that he was gone.

Within minutes, Malik had managed to turn my whole world upside down. I felt lower than scum. My heart had been broken, my ego diminished, my character compromised, yet again, and not to mention the embarrassment of my neighbors hearing all my business. Desperately, I longed to crawl into a shell and die. I didn't know where to begin to pick up the pieces of my shattered life, and wasn't sure if I wanted to.

He said all he had to say, without regard to how it made me feel, or all the time we had spent together. The countless times we made what I thought was love. Oh no, he was not gonna get off that easy. He had to pay for all the bullshit I'd been through with him and for him. Whatever his punishment, it had to be maliciously thought through. He could not see it coming. He could not be allotted preparation for it. The one thing men always griped about was how emotionally unstable women were; therefore, they should also know that fucking with our emotions can and often does become very dangerous. Malik apparently missed that memo, but he was about to have a crash course in what to do, and what not to do when it came to matters of the heart. It's true what they say: It is a thin line between love and hate. And he had crossed over to the hate side.

Chapter Eighteen

Hours had passed, as I laid within the confines of my bedroom reflecting on the day's events. How could I have once loved someone so cruel? I was at a lost. My mind couldn't rest, as I thought of poor Ariel. I felt awful. After all, I was the one who invited her back to my place. I put her in harms way. This was entirely my fault. I wanted to call her and apologize, but I wasn't sure if her number was still the same. Even if it was, I didn't know what I'd say to her. Maybe its best if I just left well enough alone, I thought to myself. If the roles were reversed, I wouldn't accept my own phone calls either. So I decided to leave it alone.

Ring…ring… My phone was going off, but I wasn't in the mood for conversation, so I didn't answer. I let my voice mail pick it up. I wanted to be left alone. It was 2 A.M. when my phone rang again, but this time I at least checked the caller ID. It was Lexy; sadly, I didn't even want to talk to her. I wouldn't have been much fun to talk to anyway, so I ignored the call and let voicemail pick up once again. Restless, I climbed out of bed and got on the Internet to look up abortion clinics. After searching several sites, I finally stumbled upon one that seemed reasonable and that catered to the needs of the women having the procedure. Based on the information I obtained from their website, they appeared to be very concerned and empathetic towards their patient's situation. My decision was made. I settled on, A Woman's Choice Clinic.

It was 4:00 A.M. when I dragged myself back to bed. To my surprise, I was ready to fall asleep. My eyes were heavy and my mind tired. I said a little prayer to God asking for guidance and forgiveness for what I was about to do. Feeling a little comforted after my prayer, I was able to fall sound asleep within seconds of my head touching the pillow.

It was that night I had the strangest of dreams. I dreamt that I was floating through a herd of white fluffy clouds in search of something. I didn't know what I was looking for, but I felt as if I had lost something. Dressed in a flowing pearl colored gown with no visualization of my feet, I drifted timelessly as the clouds took the shape of pregnant bellies. Although in a dream state of mind, my heart still felt heavy by my burdened soul.

Sobbing uncontrollably, what appeared to be a little boy approached me saying, "Mommy please don't cry. All has been forgiven." His presence was calming and his aura pure. Fair skinned with curly jet-black hair, his smile was as wide as the sun was bright. I reached out to touch him, but he vanished right before me.

Teary eyed, I jumped up out of my sleep in a cold sweat. Nervously, I scanned my room trying to convince myself that it was all a dream. I needed to make sense of what had happened, but I couldn't. I'm not a real religious person and I don't believe in all that paranormal stuff, but the only thing that made sense was that my unborn child spoke to me from within my womb; through my dream.

"All has been forgiven," his words replayed in my mind. He had already forgiven me for what I was preparing to do; a perfect example of the unconditional love that a child bears for his/her parents.

The sun shone bright into my bedroom as my alarm went off at 7:15 A.M. With all that happened during the weekend, I had completely forgotten about work. I was certainly not in the mood to deal with anyone, so I called my assistant and advised her that I would not be in due to a sudden illness. She wished me well and hung up. In desperate need of some time to think and clear my head, I isolated myself from the outside world, spending the entire day indoors alone.

Poor Lexy was none the wiser. Should I tell her about the baby or should I just get the abortion, pretending that none of this ever happened? Decisions…decisions, I didn't know what to do. Hell, I hadn't even told my best friend, which was very rare, but I just wasn't ready. Not knowing what to do was not exactly the way to introduce a crucial situation to anyone.

After concluding my call into work, I immediately called the clinic to schedule my appointment. Unfortunately, the only appointment they had available was not until another two weeks. In no position to argue, I took the appointment offered. This was bad news. I really didn't want to wait that long. The thought of carrying Malik's offspring in my womb for two more weeks made me sick to my stomach. Regurgitation quickly on the rise, my mouth began to water. Due to my lack of nourishment, I had nothing but stomach bile to contribute to the toilet bowl...ugh. I didn't want to be pregnant anymore.

Ignoring my phone was not going as I planned. It seemed to ring minutes apart from the last time it rung. Why today? Why did everyone want to call today? To avoid pulling it out the wall, I answered a few calls that I recognized; advising everyone that I was going through a selfish phase, and needed to be left alone. For all those other people I didn't care to speak to, I was thankful for the invention of voicemail.

Telemarketers, bill collectors, and family members were the easy ones, so those were the calls that got answered. It was that damn Max and Lexy who posed a problem for me. Max with her nosey ass and Lexy being overly concerned, I knew it wasn't going be as easy to get those two to leave me alone. Between the two of them my phone would never stop ringing.

At best, I would be given a few selfish hours to be alone, but that's it. Completely knowledgeable of the outcome, I tried my luck anyway. Dialing their numbers, I was relieved when voicemail picked up for the both of them.

Two hours later, as I predicted, I got a phone call. It was Max. She was the first to respond to the messages I left earlier. Reluctantly, I answered, "Hello."

"Uh-what was that message all about? Did you really think I wasn't going to call you back? Are you OK?"

"I'm fine Max. I just need some alone time. A lot's going on in my life right now and I prefer not talk about it at this present time." I reassured her in a comforting tone without making it obvious that I was blowing her off, "Sweetie, you're my best friend and I love you, but I need this time to myself."

Hesitant, "Are you sure you OK?" she asked.

"Yes."

"OK, although I don't like it, and you know I don't like it. I'll give you some space, but you make sure you check in with me periodically, and don't be gone too long."

"I won't."

In closing she said, "I love you too Danielle. Take care."

"Thank you. I will."

Saying good-bye to her was hurtful. I had just lied to my best friend, something I had never really done before, especially with a secret this big. This type of discretion was OK with any body else, but not her. Weeping lightly, I contemplated my reaction once it came time to shut Lexy out as well. Sighing, it's almost over; one down and one to go.

Lexy would be a little harder to deal with because she was my lover. Telling her that I was going to be missing in action for some time would not go over as smoothly as it did with Max. One thing about women-on-women relationships, there was always way too many damn emotions, especially when love was involved.

It was late that evening, when Lexy finally checked her messages and returned my call. She was in between shifts at the hospital and snuck away long enough to confront me about the message I had left her. "Babe, what's going on?" she asked concerned.

"Nothing for you to worry about sweetie, I just need some alone time to think some things over in my life that's all."

Her voice trembling, "Does this have to do with our relationship?"

"Some, but not all; I'm not questioning whether or not to be with you, so please don't worry unnecessarily."

"You say that, but in the same breath, you tell me you need some alone time. If it ain't about our relationship, then I don't understand why you need to be left alone. Danielle please don't shut me out," she pleaded.

"Lexy trust me. This is not something you can help me with. If you really want to help, then allow me this time with no pressure OK?" Silence on both ends of the phone. She didn't approve, but she didn't want to argue with me either. Trying to be supportive, without being too pushy, she agreed to my isolation against her will. She assured me that if I needed her, she would be there for me, no matter the day or the time. I, in return, convinced her that our relationship was not in jeopardy, and I wasn't questioning her status in my life, rather, my status in my own life. I know she didn't want to hear that, but respectably she obliged my wishes.

Chapter Nineteen

How did I get myself in such a mess? How did my world turn upside down so fast? Even more important, how was I going to get through this, and alone? I couldn't talk to anyone, because I wasn't sure what their outcome would be. I couldn't tell Lexy, because I knew it would destroy her, and Max, forget about it. She would have my head on a platter with talk of abortion. No this was something I had to figure out by my self.

The day was long and it was raining outside, so of course, that made me even more depressed. I sat and stared out my living room window and watched all the soaring airplanes go by, each in pursuit of their separate destinations. I wondered for the very first time ever where they were going. And for a quick second, I closed my eyes and imagined that I was on one of them flying far - far away.

"Dear Father," I called out to the savoir above, "help your child," I sobbed. Praying to God and my unborn child, I asked for forgiveness, for what I was planning to do in the near future. Abortion didn't sit well with me, but honestly my world was too jacked up to even consider bringing an innocent child into it. For example, I'm knocked up by a man who I use to be in love with, and now he doesn't want anything to do with it. I've got a girlfriend who has been in the dark about my affair with this man. And to top it off, I still harbored feelings for the first woman I was ever with. Chaos didn't even begin to describe the situation I had gotten myself into.

The rest of the day was spent thinking about what I wanted and what I needed to do. I knew termination was the only true option I had, but I was still hurt that the option of keeping the baby wasn't even an option at all.

Two days of complete solitude, and I was still laid up in my apartment in the dark. I hadn't eaten or drank anything for three days. I was famished, but too lazy to get up and do anything about it.

My door buzzer rang about 11:30 A.M. It was Lexy. What was she doing here? How did she get through the security gate? I wondered. "Let me in Danielle," she demanded from the other side of the door.

Still not in the mood for company, "Lexy, please just go away."

"I'm not going anywhere. You have been locked up in this house for three days now, and it's time you talk to someone. Something's wrong and I'm not leaving until I find out what it is. Now open the damn door!" She had never spoken to me in that tone before, so I knew then she was serious.

To spare my neighbors and a potential visit from Fort Lauderdale's finest, I let her in. I swear they must have planned what they thought was an intervention, because Maxine was two steps behind Lexy, once my door was open.

Upon entrance into my condo, they both greeted me with what felt like massive bear hugs; then again I was at my weakest.

"Oh my God Danielle," they both shrieked, as they looked me from head to toe. "You are not well. Look how thin you are. Have you been eating?" The questions were shooting from every angle of the room, or at least it felt that way. My head started to spin and the lights slowly dimmed. Without notice to them or myself, my frail body hit the floor.

IV's dripped much needed water into my body, as I resumed consciousness. "Ms. Cyrus, how are you feeling?" A non-familiar voice asked. Distorted, I asked my whereabouts. "You are in Memorial West Hospital. Your friends brought you in a few hours ago. Is there anything I can get for you?" she asked.

"No…not at all thank you."

The hospital, what the fuck was I doing in the hospital? Lexy was asleep at my bedside, I vaguely noticed her silhouette from behind the bed curtains.

"Hey you," Maxine's voice echoed from across the other side of the room. "Dee…you ok? Baby girl you got to tell us what's really going on with you? You scared the shit out of us."

Tears filled my eyes, as I considered telling them both the truth. "OK Max, but wake Lexy up. I only want to say this once." Without further ado, Max leaped to where Lexy was peacefully sleeping, jarring her awake.

Knowing that I had to unmask my secret, I swallowed hard, as I opened my mouth to speak. Suddenly, a tall handsome man, dressed in a long white clinical robe, entered the room and introduced himself as Dr. Shepard. "Ms. Cyrus, we're all glad to see you're awake. You scared us for a moment." Realizing where he was heading with his small talk, I tried to stop him. But before I could, he had already said too much. "The baby's fine, but you need to take better care of yourself in the future."

They both turned and looked at me with squinted eyes and brows raised. There was an awkward silence in the room. By the look on Dr. Shepard's face he knew he had revealed a deeply hidden secret. Disgusted I said, "thank you doctor, now, if you don't mind, I need a moment with my friends." Shameful of what he had done, like a dog with his tale between his legs, he lowered his head and exited the room.

I knew the both of them were looking at me, waiting for an explanation, but like a child about to be chastised, I slowly lifted my head to make eye contact. Just as expected, Lexy was teary eyed. She obviously knew she wasn't the baby daddy, so confused, she stared aimlessly at me. Max was in a frozen state of shock. Baffled by what they both heard, any further procrastination would only do more harm. Uneasy, and heavy heartedly, once again, I opened up my closet, allowing my skeletons to pour out.

Lexy seemed emotionless, as I pleaded my case. When I was done, silence took over the room once again. I analyzed Lexy's disposition as she sat in silence. "You're pregnant?" She finally spoke. "You're fucking pregnant! You were fucking a man and fucking me? The same lips that pleasured me in ways that made me feel was just for me, pleasured someone else? Pregnant...Danielle," she screamed!

When Lexy and I first met, she forewarned me that she didn't work well under emotional distress. She was prone to hives during extremely stressful times. Hyperventilating, she broke out in a cold sweat and I noticed that her neck was gradually turning red. "Calm down Lexy, please calm down," Maxine encouraged; trying not to become panicked herself.

I didn't know what to do or say. I reached for her, but she pulled away. "Danielle, I have to get her out of here." Lexy said, "I have to go now, before I do or say something I may live to regret." With no goodbyes, they both exited the room. First Lexy exited then Max. I felt like a monster for what I had done to her. She didn't deserve this. Through the stale colored corridor walls, I could still hear her screams, although they were becoming fainter. Assuming they both had deserted me; I rolled to my side and cried, staring out the window.

How many times could one heart break? Knowing that I hurt someone so close to me, broke my heart into micro mini pieces. I knew she felt the ultimate betrayal. I wanted so much to run after her, but I knew at that moment the safest place for me to be was right where I was-in my hospital bed. Lexy wasn't a violent person, but right now I didn't want to test the waters. Chaos had truly taken over my world. How did I get here, I kept asking myself? One minute I was on top of my game. I had a smart, good-looking man and a woman who made heads turn everywhere she went. Now, look at me, alone and lonely; deserted in a cold hospital room with damn needles going through my veins.

My phone rung as I wiped tears from my eyes, hoping it was Lexy. Hurriedly, I answered, "Hello."

"Good evening Ms. Cyrus." The voice on the other end sang. Way too chipper to be anyone I knew at this present moment.

"Yes, this is Ms. Cyrus."

"Sorry to interrupt you, but this is A Woman's Choice clinic calling about your appointment for next week. We actually had a cancellation and wanted to offer you a sooner appointment, if you're interested in coming in earlier."

"Oh-Um, yes, when and what time?" I asked mentally distorted.

"Tomorrow at 2 P.M. Is that OK with you?"

"Yeah, that's perfect."

"Great, we'll see you then. Remember to get plenty of sleep and try not to worry. The procedure will go smoothly. Well, have a good evening."

"Thanks." I said a little confused. *Did she think this was a regular office visit for me? Calling like this was a happy event or something.* I almost snapped on her, as I thought of this, but instead, I cordially said goodbye and hung up. She wasn't the cause of my problems. She was just doing her job and wouldn't have deserved the lashing I was about to give her.

Moments after ending my call, a male nurse entered the room with a dinner tray. For hospital food it smelled really good. Then again, I hadn't eaten in several days. "Here you go Ms. Cyrus, please let me know if you need anything else." Lifting my head rest, he placed the tray in front of me. Destined to feel better so I could get out of the hospital, I forced myself to eat something before I turned in for the night. The quicker I went to sleep, the quicker I could go home and make it to my appointment tomorrow. Soon this would all be over, and I could get back to my normal life. As fucked up as it was…it was still my life. I just wanted what was normal to me back, excluding Malik of course.

Chapter Twenty

The next morning, I woke up in discontentment due to another sleepless night. With all that had been going on, it wore heavy on my conscious. I had another dream about my unborn child, or what I took as dreams of my unborn child. There was a huge abandoned building and I was standing by myself, looking at the walls covered in graffiti. I remember the feeling of being cold because the building was drafty, damp, and dark. The faint sound of an infant in despair drew me towards the direction of the crying. The closer I appeared to be getting to the sound the further in distance the voice became.

Blind to the reason behind the crying, I had a keen urge to find the hurting child. I wasn't sure if the child was in danger or not, but the thought consumed me, fueling my efforts to locate the infant. Overwhelmed, I called out to the whimpering baby, but to no avail. Panicked, I began running and looking for the little person in need. Bend after bend, empty corner, after corner; exhausted, I was about to give up my search. Then, an image appeared before me out of nowhere. Admirably, I stood face to face with the most beautiful pair of sparkling brown eyes I had ever seen. Angelic, he posed no threat. Although a stranger to me, there was something familiar about him. I had seen this little boy before, I thought to myself, but where?

Unafraid, the little boy approached me, never once taking his eyes off me. He reached for my belly and I jumped a little. Not because I was afraid, it was just unexpected. I watched him as he laid hands on my womb and hovered above my unborn child. Streams of tears fell from my eyes. He was no older than five-years' old, but very wise. With a great deal of love in his voice, he whispered in my ear, "I forgive you mommy."

And before I could respond, the angelic mirage disappeared like a light mist. Once again I was left standing alone in a strange place. Shook, I jumped up out of my sleep mumbling the word alone. Forgetting where I was, I looked around the cramped room and realized I was truly alone. No Max, no Lexy, no one.

Lying back down in my hospital bed, there was no mistaking it. I knew that face and that voice. I've seen and heard it before in a previous dream. My unborn son had reached out to me, yet again from within my womb. So badly shook, I really wanted to call Lexy and talk to her about my dreams, but I wouldn't have been strong enough for the both of us. So instead, I told myself to just deal with it. After all, I was the only one responsible for me being in this fucked up predicament. And as the old saying goes, "I made my bed, now it was time to lay in it."

Determined, I shook that nervous feeling in the pit of my stomach, got up out of bed, and got dressed. I had no time to wait for a formal release from the hospital. Time was ticking and I had business to take care of.

Leaving from the hospital in a cab, I asked the driver to turn the radio off; I wanted complete silence. For the first time ever, I took heed to the numerous billboards that advertised abortions as we sped past them. I swear, out of every five there was at least one about unplanned pregnancy rights. Whether it was pro abortions or against them, the advertisement was apparent.

It's funny how you never seem to notice things, until it was you in that particular situation. Like how you would never pay attention to a certain kind of car, until you or someone you knew had one. Then all of a sudden they were seen everywhere. Well, that's how my ride home to pick up my car was.

After I paid my cab fare, I got in my car and turned on the ignition. I didn't bother to go inside my condo at all. What I had worn to the hospital the other day was exactly what I had on at that present moment. Turning the ignition, I gripped the steering wheel tightly as I revved the engine lightly. The moment of truth had arrived. *Now or never,* I thought to myself.

Buzz…buzz…My cell vibrated with a text message from Lexy reminding me of how much she loved me. Surprised, but grateful; I really needed to hear that. It was good to know that someone still cared for me, especially after what I had done. Smiling, I placed my phone back in its holster. I didn't see the need to reply. I headed toward the clinic.

The drive to A Woman's Choice was over 45 minutes from my house, but I finally arrived just in time for my appointment. I chose one far away from home on purpose. I didn't want anyone to recognize me. The less people in my immediate surroundings knew of me, the better. I didn't want to be labeled the "baby killer." Although my embryo was still just a small clot, most abortion advocates didn't understand or care about the mother's reasoning behind the termination and would bad mouth them anyway. That being the case, I had too much at stake if this was to ever get out. Career wise, the media would have eaten me up, possibly causing me my job. Million-dollar, A-list clients, would no longer want to be associated with a company that condoned abortions, so discretion was a must.

Pulling up to the clinic, I didn't feel like I was in the right place. The outside appearance was misleading, or at least it was to me. From the looks of it, you wouldn't assume that they performed abortion procedures. It looked real nice, and well maintained like any other doctors office. Honestly, I expected an old beat up building with the paint chipping off, graffiti sprayed all over it, and several pissy drunk homeless vagrants standing around asking for loose change. OK, so I watch a lot of TV.

Speaking of TV, previously on a popular talk show, I had heard horrible horror stories about abortions gone wrong; remembering that, made me a little paranoid. I didn't know what to expect, so I expected the worst and hoped for the best. Relieved by the pleasant ambiance of the clinic, I knew the possibility of me walking out disease free and in one piece was extremely high.

I said a little prayer like I always did whenever I was faced with uncertainties and stepped inside. I ain't gon' lie, I was more nervous than a person incarcerated for the first time. In fact, I was scared shitless.

Inside the clinic smelled of fresh pine and bleach. That was the signature aroma of an immaculate health facility. Walking in, I expected to hear screaming, but there wasn't any. Goes to show you can't believe everything you see or hear on TV. Approaching the frosted glass window that hid the receptionist, "Hello, you must be Ms. Cyrus?" A young attractive woman said, while grabbing a clip board and pen.

"Yeah, how did you know?"

"Well its 1:55 P.M. and your appointment is at 2:00 P.M. Since this is an appointment only facility, I took a guess." she smiled. Although she was being a smart ass, she was kind of cute, so I didn't get curt with her. "Here, I need you to fill these papers out. When you're done, I will check you in." She handed me the clipboard stacked with papers so thick, that I thought she handed me a small manuscript for review.

Taking a seat in one of the many wood framed chairs, I began reading the first of many policy disclosures. As I looked up to give my eyes a rest, I noticed all the baby pictures neatly organized on the wall. Not to mention, all the baby books that were laid about the tables in the office. A bit backwards if you ask me. This was an abortion clinic, so why promote life, when apparently this was a practice to take life away? I began to feel uneasy, as I thought about my dream last night and the possibility of this being my only chance of being a mother. My palms began to sweat and I started to feel really ill.

Observant and concerned about the sudden paleness in my face, "Are you OK, Ms Cyrus?" the receptionist asked, peeking over her counter.

"Yes, I'm fine." I lied. Where's your water fountain?"

"Down the hall to your left," she buzzed me through the double doors and visually directed me in the direction of the fountain.

Slowly walking down the seemingly long hallway, I passed lots of exam rooms on either side of me; it looked more like a hospital hallway than a clinic. The walls were painted that awful olive green color and the climate was extremely cold. Rooms were labeled per there purpose: Exam room, triage room, procedure room, recovery room and observation room. Didn't know the process had that many steps to it.

Approaching my destination, there was one room door slightly ajar. Inside, I could hear a young girl whimpering to her mother, begging for immunity. "Mom I don't want to do this. I want my child. How could you ask me to do this when you didn't abort me? I can't mom. I just can't. I want my child," sobbing, she continued to plead with her unmovable mother. Petrified, she didn't sound anymore than 16 years old. Then the door shut, and I heard another voice, a male voice, must have been the doctor. His voice was soothing. Although I couldn't make out his words, I knew he was trying to convince the frightened girl that this was the best thing for her, and that everything was going to be OK.

"Ma'am," the cute receptionist interrupted, "I'm sorry, but I need to get you checked in and record your vitals. Are you ready?"

"Uh-yeah," I said nervously. Hoping she hadn't noticed me snooping. Truth was, I was more unsure then, than I was when I first got here. That girl's sobbing, along with my dreams and the many baby photos hanging around the office began to haunt me. Confused, and growing more undecided by the minute, part of me wanted to run out, while the other part threatened me to stay.

The room marked triage is where the medical assistant commenced her normal check of my vitals. Blood pressure, temperature, respirations, pulse, etc. "OK, follow me Ms Cyrus. I will take you to the examination room, where the doctor will talk with you in more detail about the procedure. After hearing all he has to say, and getting a better understanding of what to expect, you can then decide if you want to go through with it or not. At that time, if you decide to stay, we will then take payment from you; the consultation of course is free. Are there any questions for me?" she asked, as she passed me a changing slip.

"No. Thank you." Closing the door behind her, I scanned the room in search of a distraction; anything that would take my mind off current events.

The sterile room was already pre-prepped with all sorts of gadgets, instruments of all kinds, most of which, I had never seen, or imagined would be present in a doctor's office. I wasn't sure if this set up was preparation for an abortion or for a tune up on a car. The shit was scary. Why would they purposely leave the instruments out for patients to see was beyond me. As indecisive as I had become, the doctor had better hurry up before I changed my mind completely, I thought to myself.

To aid with my approximate gestation, there was a sonogram machine to the back of the cold bland room. Most of the instruments on the mayo stand, I recognized from routine Pap Smears, but others were straight out hideous. Panicked, I wanted out of that room. I was not quite at the cut off mark for legal abortions yet, so I had more time to think about it. Decided, I began to gather my things to leave, and then there was a knock from the other side of door and in walked the doctor.

He was a short bulky man in his mid to late 40's. "Ms Cyrus, how are you today?" He asked with a flirtatious grin on his face.

"Apparently not good, if I'm in your office wouldn't you say?" I snapped.

"I see. Well try to relax. The procedure is virtually painless. Anesthesia is provided to help you with the discomfort and cramping. I will have you out of here in less then two hours, but first I need to find out how far along you are. Then we'll go from there."

Pleased with his briefing, he instructed me to lie on the table. He performed the sonogram and I was shocked at the image on the screen. Although the silhouette was not very big in size, it was present, and living within me. I couldn't believe it, there was my baby, growing within my womb. Looking at the monitor, he told me I was 10 weeks, which was exactly 2 ½ months. Then there was a loud thump boom, boom, like the sound of a heart beating.

"What is that?" I asked.

"It's the baby's heart beat," he responded.

Staring at the screen, this was all too surreal. The sound of my baby's heart beating complicated things even more. As I listened to the sweet melody that confirmed life, I entertained the thought of being a mother and the whole idea of abortion no longer felt right to me.

"Alright, any questions?" The doctor asked snapping me back into reality. Unbeknownst to him, he had been carrying on a conversation by himself for some time now.

"So are we ready to begin Ms. Cyrus?" he asked, anxious to proceed.

"Uh, actually doc, I think I need some more time to think about this. Before seeing my baby on the ultrasound, I was sure this was what I wanted to do, but now I'm not too sure. How long do I have before it's too late?" I inquired.

"To be honest Ms. Cyrus, you only have about two more weeks before I can no longer perform the procedure. You would then have to go to another facility; a practice that performs abortions past three months."

"I understand, but I just can't do this right now. I need more time. Thanks anyway doc, but I have to go."

Quickly, I leaped off the table and without a moments notice, began wiping the sonogram jelly off my belly. Rushing down the corridor, past the receptionist area, I was out of that doctor's office quicker than a cat could lick his behind.

What was happening to me? Was I really considering going all the way with this kid or was I having a nervous breakdown? Why did I smile to myself when I saw the image on the sonogram? Why was the thought of being a mother slowing becoming a reality that I was accepting of? Questions...questions... so many of them, but still no real definite answers. *Wait a minute...Could this-do I really? Damn! I think I had finally developed a love for my unborn child.*

Chapter Twenty-One

I had no idea what I was doing. It was all so crazy to me. I had decided to keep my child and do the best I could for him or her. And being that I was still in my first trimester, I knew it was best to not broadcast my condition to anyone. At least not until the second trimester, which was considered being past the danger zone. I had read somewhere that if the pregnancy was not a viable one that the body would rid itself of it within the first trimester and so for my body was accepting of it, but still I wanted to keep the pregnancy a secret just in case.

I thought it would be better to let everyone continue to think that I had gotten the abortion; everyone except for Lexy. I was kind of hoping that she would want to be a part of my pregnancy. Nowhere was it written in law that a kid needed both a mother and a father to have an honest upbringing. In my opinion, two loving mothers could provide the same level of love and support for a child as any heterosexual couple.

A week had passed since Lexy had stormed out of the hospital. I allowed her some space to think over all that had transpired, before confronting her again with another obstacle to overcome. Though I wanted her forgiveness, I didn't want to rush her, so I kept my distance. In the mean time, I sent her roses and a four-page letter apologizing for all my screw ups. Although she never responded to either gesture, I knew or should I say, I felt that she knew how sincere I was and appreciated that. There was nothing left for me to do, but wait on a response from her. Until then, I worked on me, and prepared for the arrival of my child.

Over the next few months my body had changed so drastically. I went from a coca-cola shape, to a damn pear shape overnight. My belly had grown so much and the baby moved non-stop. I never knew a joy like this before. Feeling another life move around inside me was utterly priceless. The first time my baby moved it scared the shit out of me. I was watching TV and got the munchies, so I grabbed me some fruit and a tall glass of cold water. As soon as I drank that glass of water, my stomach started to take a weird shape. I looked down and saw what looked like little limbs grazing across my stomach underneath my skin. It freaked me out so bad, but thanks to my "What to Expect When You're Expecting" book, I was calmed. It explained that that was just my child moving and stretching. I was relieved. He/she has not stopped moving since that day. And Lexy had finally come around… hooray!

It took her a good two months, but she forgave me and we agreed to work on our relationship. In an attempt at a new start, we mutually agreed to have a confessional, unveiling any and all secrets that we had been keeping from one another. This was an open forum for all questions to be asked, as well as answered.

She wanted to know all about my affair with Malik, and my one night with Ariel the night Malik caught us. The hurt in her eyes broke me down internally. Telling her all my dirty little secrets was one of the hardest things I ever had to do. It made me realize how much of an idiot I had been. I had the perfect love with Lexy, and I almost killed that by fucking around with Malik and Ariel. I was so over that part of my life. I wanted nothing more than to raise my child with the woman that I finally realized I had loved all along.

Initially, she sobbed for a while like I expected her to, but what I didn't expect was for her to be so empathetic and forgiving of me. She told me that she had never experienced a hurt like that before, but even more so, she had never experienced love for anyone like she felt for me. She explained to me that she too, had made mistakes in her life. Although faithful to me, she had cheated on someone in her past. It's because of that person's forgiveness that she was able and willing to forgive me.

She believed that everyone deserved, and was worthy of a second chance as long as their heart was truly remorseful. She warned me that this was my last chance. Should I fuck it up, she would then move on with her life; content with knowing that she deserved much better than what I had to offer. Grateful for her forgiveness, I promised her that nothing like what's happened in my past would ever happen again.

We agreed to take things slower this time. We would start by talking on the phone and gradually incline to going out on dates; dates that would end at the car, instead of in one of our beds. Then over time, as her heart mended, we would advance to more intimate encounters. I may have been forgiven, but she had definitely not forgotten.

Four months had passed and I was in my third trimester. To be exact, I was then eight months pregnant, and as big as a house. Max had been let in on my secret back when I was around five months. It was no way of hiding it anymore. My belly had started to take on its basketball shape during the fourth and fifth month of gestation, and I was as round as all outdoors. Lexy was sweet about it though. She reminded me everyday of how beautiful she thought I was. That really did boost my esteem, because I had never weighed more than 130 pounds in all my life. But at least it was almost over. Soon I would be back in my size six, hopefully.

Although things between Lexy and I were cool, I was still bothered, because I hadn't told Malik that I kept the baby. He was still the biological father whether he liked it or not. I didn't want anything from him by far; I just felt he deserved to know. There was an awful feeling to my gut, as I thought about telling him. Reminiscing on how he responded last time, made my skin crawl and my stomach upset. But he had the right to know. Lexy was against it, but she understood my position. She offered to come with me if I decided to tell him, but I convinced her that things would surely go bad if she were present.

A dead, cold feeling consumed by body as a familiar, yet, undesired voice answered when I called. "Malik, this is Danielle."

"I know who this is. It hasn't been that long. Let me guess, you miss big daddy don't you?" I wanted to barf at the thought.

"No. Hell no! I was calling you because I need to talk to you about something important. I was wondering if we could meet up for coffee."

"Sure, just tell me when and where."

The fact that he wasn't concerned about why I wanted to meet him, bothered me a little, but I just shook it off and replied, "We can meet at the coffee house on Collins Ave tomorrow around 10:00 A.M."

"That's fine with me Danielle. Oh by the way, wear my favorite Chanel dress. The one I brought you for our anniversary. You know the one with the low cut in the front that holds your breast perfectly." Chuckling, "Yeah, you know the one that stops at your thighs, revealing those sexy ass yellow legs of yours. Put that one on for me OK?"Grossed out beyond recognition, I just said goodbye and hung up.

That one conversation with him turned my stomach one too many times. The nerve of that bastard; he actually thought I would do as he asked of me. Like nothing ever happened between us. It was official; Malik was psychotic.

Chapter Twenty-Two

Now that I was on maternity leave from work, Lexy had taken up more hours at the hospital, as if she wasn't working long enough hours already. She said that she wanted the best for her family by any means necessary; she also wanted to be able to stay home with me for the first six months after birth. I didn't like the idea of her working so much, but I knew it was for a good cause. Besides, her being home with me for six months was reward enough in its self. Patience was truly a virtue.

Not working was so over rated. I didn't understand how people could go so long purposely, not working. I'd only been out of work for a few weeks and I had already started to miss it. Being at home, all I did all day was eat, watch TV, masturbate, eat some more, and drive myself crazy thinking about Lexy. Wondering when she was coming home.

Eventually, we had moved in with each other to save on rent. Since my place was bigger, and in a better location, she moved in with me. Surprisingly, we hadn't already moved in with one another, since that seemed to be the way of lesbians. First they meet, date for a month or two, then next thing you know… an instant family. Gay relationships were more accelerated than heterosexual ones. Our emotions grew at a phenomenal rate, or at least that had been my experience with it.

Ring, ring "Hey big belly," Max said.

"Hey girl," I replied.

"So how's my God child doing today?"

"She's good, kicking the hell out of me. (I had found out during my 5th month that it was a girl) What are you up too?"

"I was going shopping for the baby and wanted to know if you cared to come along?"

"Um, maybe next time. I'm feeling kind of worn out today."

"You always say that shit. You know if I didn't love you, and my God child so much, I would come kick your lazy ass right on out the front door. All you do is eat, sleep, and shit."

"Don't forget masturbate," I teased.

"Yeah, that too, ole nasty heifer. You better be careful, or your ass gone blow up just like a damn whale and that's when I won't claim your ass no more."

"That's OK; Lexy will still love me in all my glory. And stop your lying. You know you would love all of me; no matter how obnoxiously big I got."

Laughing, "You're right Shamu-you're right," she agreed. "Bye crazy, I got shopping to do. Love ya and I'll talk to you later."

"Love you too."

It was around 7:30 P.M. when I got off the phone with Max. I had to hurry up. Lexy usually got home around 9:00 P.M., and I needed to shower, clean, cook, and make my fat ass look presentable to her. I really didn't have to do all that, but I had a thing about not letting her come home with me looking the exact same way I did when she left. I didn't want her to grow tired of me, so I made sure every time she came home, I was dressed to impress, pregnant and all.

We had been shopping, so I had some pretty sexy maternity clothes. Who ever said you couldn't be sexy while pregnant, never met me. Going the extra mile, I even styled my hair differently just about every other day. I had to remind her of the beauty she had waiting for her at home.

It was 8:53 P.M. when I heard Lexy at the door. My heart always sped up when I knew she was coming. Every time I saw her, was like seeing her the first time. I thought that to be the cutest thing. The aroma of pasta and garlic lingered in the air, as she walked through the door. "Good evening baby," she said, as she tiredly kissed my cheek. "How are both my babies?"

"We're fine," I said, with a girlish grin.

"How was work today?"

"Oh baby, I don't want to talk about work right now. I've missed you all day. The only thing on my mind at this moment is making love to the most beautiful, sexy woman, ever created."

Without a second thought, I dropped what I was doing, turned dinner down to a simmer, and was in the bedroom, half naked, before she could finish what she was saying. With loving like hers she didn't have to ask, or even imply but once.

Watching her as she undressed, her body never looked more beautiful. She hadn't changed at all, unlike me. I still had a pretty face, but Lord knows my body had seen better days. Sensing my insecurities about my body, she came over to me and kissed me from head to toe; being especially careful not to miss a single inch. In an effort to boost my esteem, she said, "I never knew that a pregnant woman could be so sexy, but baby pregnancy looks damn good on you. I realize the life growing inside of you and that enables me to fall deeper and deeper in love with you. This is our baby you're carrying, no matter the conception. We are a family, and I love the both of you dearly."

Speaking those words, she became one with my body. It was at that moment that I fell completely in love with Lexy.

Morning had come so fast. Last night was beautiful. Lexy and I connected with one another with great passion and intensity. And as much as I didn't want her to go to work, I needed her to go. This was the day I agreed to met up with Malik. Lord, I hope you're watching over me today. I don't know how Malik is going react, I prayed.

I arrived at the coffee shop around 9:45 A.M. I wanted to get there early, so I could already be sitting when he got there. I ordered myself a hot chocolate and anxiously awaited his arrival. It was 10:05 A.M. when I looked up from my daze and spotted Malik walking towards me. Boy was I nervous.

"Well, hello Ms. Cyrus, how are you?" he said, gesturing to kiss my cheek.

"Happy," I curtly responded, turning my cheek away from him. This was not a social call and we were not friends.

"I see your still a lil' bitter, but don't be mad at me baby. That's in the past. We're here now, in the present, and possibly the future."

"I see you're still a jack ass and as full of yourself as you've always been, so I'll make this real quick." Taking a deep breath, "Malik," I started, as a waiter asking for Malik's beverage order interrupted me.

"What can I get you sir?" The tall gentleman asked.

"I'll take a large coffee, black, with two sugars," he responded.

"And you ma'am?"

"I'm good, thank you." The waiter walked away and I continued, "Malik, there's something I think you should know," hands sweating, nerves shot, I proceeded, "remember the last argument we had, the one that finalized our break up?"

"Yeah, I try to forget about it. I know I said some pretty fucked up shit to you. I mean I was pissed. That whole pregnancy thing just wasn't expected. And I'm sorry that I didn't come with you to the doctor, but you know how crazy things were between us back then."

"It's OK," I said, as I inhaled deeply then exhaled. "About the doctor I…."

"Sir, here's your coffee." I was once again interrupted. "Would you like to pay now or later?"

"Now is fine, how much do I owe you?"

"$2.85 sir," the waiter said, handing Malik a piece of paper. "Do you need change?" he asked as Malik handed him payment.

I was on the verge of pissing my pants; I had to say what was on my mind before I had a nervous breakdown, so out of frustration I yelled, "No, damn it! Just keep the fucking change and don't come back over here." And with my second breath I blurted out, "I didn't get the abortion and I'm almost nine months pregnant." Then I exhaled.

Silence filled the air. I felt as if the whole coffee house froze in time, as I awaited his reaction. Judging from the expression on his face, I knew he too, was trying to decide just how to react. Cracking his neck, he rubbed his visually throbbing temples then fixated his eyes on me. "Two things: first, that was a $50 dollar bill I handed that server. And second, what the fuck you mean you still pregnant? Are you trying to get hurt?" His body language changed and he instantly became that man from several months ago, who mentally and physically abused me in my own home. Once again I was frightened.

Malik rose from the table, took account of his surroundings, and moved closer to where I remained seated. "If you touch me, that's a felony; punishable by prison time," I reminded him. Leaning his head down close enough, so that only I could hear the gut piercing words coming from his mouth. He touched the top of my belly and said, "Oh, I ain't gon touch you, at least not yet. But I assure you Danielle, one way or the other, this bastard child of yours will be terminated!"

Acting as if nothing had happened, he got up, kissed my cheek, and walked away. I was frozen stiff. Feeling light headed and faint, all pigmentation escaped from my skin. My heart rate accelerated and my palms started to sweat. Because I was unsettled, the effects spiraled down to my baby causing her to move frantically. That's when I knew it was time to calm down. Unintentionally, I had transferred my stress to my child, which was not a good thing, since stress has been proven to be detrimental to an unborn child.

Trying to calm down, I sat for a long period of time after Malik had left. I sang nursery rhymes and rocked back and forth in hopes of calming both me and the baby. When her movements finally simmered down to a non-threatening pace, I gathered myself to leave. But not before I apologized to the server for my rude behavior earlier, then I congratulated him on his biggest tip of the day. Exiting the coffee shop, the dry air swept across my face, drying the streams of tears that had fallen. Malik had really hurt me with how harsh spoke to me, but I chose to tell him. That was my fault. I should've known better.

Lexy was right, he didn't need to know. This was going to be our baby, hers and mine, and he really didn't have a part in it. To keep the peace in my home, I knew it was best to leave the threatening part of our conversation out. I would just tell her that Malik stood me up. That way, she wouldn't be upset or nervous thinking that he was going to harm me or the baby. Damn, here I was again keeping secrets. I felt like shit, for even contemplating not telling her. No more lies Danielle, I reminded myself. I will tell her, just not today. I was already riled up enough for the both of us. Somebody had to be calm and collected. I'd tell her tomorrow.

Chapter Twenty-Three

It was Friday morning, time for my weekly doctor's appointment. I jumped up out of bed excited. It had been a couple of weeks since my encounter with Malik and nothing had happened. I knew he was full of hot air. Either way, I had already told Lexy about my meeting with him and his obviously empty threat. She was frantic just as I expected; she literally wanted to kill him. Not knowing for sure whether he was truly capable of doing any of the things he so violently promised, I still told her; blindly, assuring her that he was only talking shit and couldn't hurt a fly. I'm glad she believed my optimism, because I wasn't so confident about what I told her myself. I only hoped it was true.

Ring, ring… "Good morning sweetheart," Lexy sang to me. "How are both my babies doing?"

"We're fine, about to leave for the doctor's office."

"You know I hate that I'm not able to go with you today. I just couldn't get the coverage for my shift, but I want blow by blow details on how the visit goes."

Fumbling through the kitchen in search of something to eat, "Yes, babe. I know how much it bothers you to not be going, but I will give you an update when you get home. We're gonna miss you."

"Same here, I got to go. Drive safe, I love you."

"I love you too boo. Have a good day at work."

The doctor's office was packed as usual. Dr. Hannah was better known than I originally thought. Max was the one who told me about him. She told me that an ex of hers' sister was his patient during her pregnancy and he was awesome. Dr. Hannah was genuinely compassionate towards his patients. His involvement went beyond standard medical practice; he actually cared for each and every one of his patients.

Unlike other doctors that I've had the displeasure of meeting, Dr. Hannah was a professional in his approach and had very caring bedside manners. He was so different from the typical money driven physicians who cared more about how much they could bill for a particular visit, versus focusing on providing quality healthcare; no matter what the reason for the visit. I never cared for that type of doctor. And don't forget about the ones that would come into the room, barely speak to you, and then start putting instruments inside your bodily orifices with no forewarning. No, not Dr. Hannah, he took his time. He explained in great detail everything he was about to do to you as his patient. That way, there were never any unwelcomed surprises.

He was a true professional, not cold hearted or money driven. Yes, his practice thrived off of financial substance, but it was his warmth that kept him abundantly wealthy. Most physicians don't realize that doctors come a dime a dozen, and it's all in the way they treat their patients that determines their success. Dr. Hannah was different, and he understood that his patients were his livelihood and treated them as such.

At the check in counter I was greeted by Asia, one of the doctor's medical assistants. "Hey Danielle," she said. She wasn't quite my age, but she was of legal age. I had no doubt that she was "family" by the way she flirted with me at every single visit. She was one of the cuter ones that worked there, and I entertained her sly advances. Clearly she was deep in her closet, but twisted nonetheless.

I was pregnant, but shit, I still looked good. "Hey baby girl," I responded.

My wait to be seen was no longer than twenty minutes. That was the average wait time. Due to how crowded the office was, I was prepared to wait even longer. Escorted by Asia, we entered the small exam room. Triaging me, she took my vital signs and recorded any changes in my history since my last visit. She weighed me in and purposely pressed her twenty year old breast firmly against my arm, as she stood slightly to the side of me. Being a woman who loved breast, naturally, I was a little turned on-OK, a lot turned on. *This lil' girl had better sit down somewhere 'for she got what she was after,* I thought to myself for a split second, and then I remembered Lexy.

The devil was busy at work; I couldn't help but notice the erection of her moderately sized nipples. I didn't think it was cold enough in the cramped room to warrant such a rise, so my only assumption was that her nipples were hard because she was turned on. "Where's Lexy today?" she asked as if she really cared.

"Working, she wanted to be here, but couldn't get the coverage at work."

"I see," she said, recording something in my chart. "Some people don't realize what they have until it's gone. If you were my woman, there's no way you would be sitting here alone. Lexy better wake up, there's always someone willing to pick up where she slacks off."

Aha! Confirmed, I knew she was a lesbian! I was flattered. There I was, nine months pregnant, and she had come on to me. Taking my blood pressure, she positioned herself right in front of me; straddling one of my legs in between hers. She was sexy as hell; I tried not to feed into what she was doing. With her "V" staring me in the face, I could smell the scent of her excited pussy creeping from beneath her scrub pants. Inhaling her, our bodies were linked with one another. Instantly, my pussy too, became wet, as thoughts of her being naked invaded my thoughts. Temptation seeking to get the best of me, and winning, I reached for her leg.

Unannounced, "Any complaints today Ms. Cyrus?" Dr. Hannah asked, as he entered the room.

Startled, yet relieved at the same time, "No doctor, just ready to have this baby." We all laughed. For Asia and I, it was an uncomfortable laugh. She must've felt as bad as I did for what almost happened; just moments, before the doctor walked in the door.

"Three more weeks Ms. Cyrus," he smiled, as he commenced with his OB check. Squeezing the sonogram gel onto my stomach, he listened to the baby's heartbeat with his doppler. "Every thing sounds fine and looks great; however, I still need to do an internal exam, seeing that you are so close to your due date." Handing me a paper drape to conceal my nakedness, he and Asia exited the room to allow me to change.

When he came back in the room, I was happy to see that it was Asia who escorted him. It was her face that I wanted to focus on, as he inserted his fingers into my horniness. I wanted her to watch and imagine it was her fingers that fucked me slowly. "OK, relax; I'm beginning the exam now," Dr. Hannah forewarned. I was the last person he needed to tell to relax. He extended his gloved hand out and waited for Asia to squeeze some gel onto his two fingers. Lubrication was not really necessary, I was already moist.

Upon insertion, I gasped, damn near came, as he pushed his thick long fingers deep into my pussy, searching for my cervix. Usually, these kinds of exams were extremely uncomfortable, and Lexy would have to hold my hand, but not today. I didn't need any added support. This time it was quite pleasurable, considering, my mind was on Asia and not the doctor.

A silent moan crept out, and Asia's eyes were fixated directly on me. Gently biting down on her bottom lip, she lowered her eyes in ecstasy—slightly closing them. What we were doing was so wrong, on so many levels, but we were too far gone to stop it. I was literally dripping; painfully wanting to cum. Asia still within my view, my warm wetness slowly ran down to the crack of my ass, as I silently came all over Dr. Hannah's gloved fingers. "Are you leaking amniotic fluid Ms. Cyrus?" The doctor asked, noticing that I was drenched in clear liquid.

"No doctor. Not that I know of," I shamefully replied.

"Oh, OK. Well all is good, but don't hesitate to call me if you should start having contractions."

"OK, I will."

As a doctor, I'm sure he knew that I had cum, versus leaked amniotic fluid. But being the professional that he was, he maintained his composure.

What happened during my examination had never happened to me before. Apparently, it had never happened to Asia before either. She looked a little freaked out, but her exhausted body language exemplified a satisfied woman; a woman who had just reached her sexual climax. Embarrassed, yet content; I attempted to wipe away the aroma of sex by using a wet nap located on the countertop in the exam room. Once dressed, I followed my doctor's instructions and scheduled my next appointment before exiting the back office area.

The parking lot was still full of cars, which left me searching for mine. Being that the garage was so damn big, I could never find my exact parking space. I remembered parking my car on the third floor, but looking up at the painted number on the pole, I happened to be aimlessly strolling around on the fourth floor. Appreciating the exercise, I decided to walk down one level, instead of getting back on the elevator. It was light outside, but still a little dark in the garage. As I walked down to third level, I couldn't shake the feeling that I wasn't alone. I had seen enough movies in my day to know that when you had the feeling you were being followed, you probably were.

Frantically scrambling through my purse in search of my keys, I cursed myself for not already having them out. A person should always have their keys easily accessible, especially in a parking garage. Finally spotting my car off in the distance, I felt a sense of relief. Then out of nowhere, I heard a second set of footsteps, which made me overly eager to get inside my car. My once steady pace, quickly turned into a light jog, and so did the second set of footsteps. This wasn't a case of simple paranoia; I was being followed. My heart was beating fast; too afraid to turn around, I ran faster.

Running with a seven pound person inside my belly was not easy, but I did the best I could.

With my key in the keyhole, I was about to pull the door handle, when suddenly, I was attacked from behind. His chest was firmly pressed against my back, one arm was tightly around my neck, and his filthy hand covered my mouth, "Bitch you were warned, but you wouldn't listen. See what happens when you don't do as you're told. You did this to yourself."

Reaching over my head, I clawed at his face, in an attempt to defend myself. My attempts subsided as something sharp pierced deeply into my side; penetrating through the layers of my skin. All I could think of was my baby as I grabbed my wound. So much blood fled from my body, as I looked around for someone to help me, but I was alone. There was no one there, not even my attacker. As quickly as he appeared, so did he disappear; leaving only the grunt sound of his voice ringing in my ear, and the cheap scent of his cologne blanketed within my clothes. Falling down onto the asphalt, I cried to my God. *"Father, please protect my baby. Lord, please."* I hysterically cried out, until I rendered into a state of unconsciousness.

Stiff and sore, I awoke hooked up to all kinds of monitoring machines and IV's in my arms. Weak and unable to focus, I barely muttered, "Where am I?"

"Relax Ms. Cyrus. Don't try to do too much," an unfamiliar voice said.

"What? Who are you? Why am I hooked up to all these damn machines?" I asked irritated.

"Well, you were involved in a horrible accident, and we're simply monitoring you for safety. You were attacked and-" He stumbled over his words. Although his lips were moving, I didn't understand a word he was saying. My focus was redirected towards the shooting pain in the lower part of my stomach.

Remembering my pregnancy, I reached down to check on my baby. Only to find that my once round belly was abnormally flat, and stapled shut.

"What…Where's my baby?" I interrupted his rambling. "Where the fuck is my baby?" I cried.

"Ms. Cyrus, please stop yelling, I've been trying to tell you that we had to perform an emergency C-section. We attempted to save both, you and your baby," voice trembling, "unfortunately, the knife to your side, pierced through the protective sac, penetrating your baby as well. We did all we could do, but we were too late. I'm so very sorry."

The room darkened, as his voice became more distant and muffled. Breathing became a difficult task, as I fought for air. Loosing that battle, I passed out. When I finally regained consciousness, I awoke to Lexy holding my hand crying.

"Lexy," I cried. "They took her. They took our angel." Trying not to break completely down, "I know baby, I know." Lexy wiped my eyes and held me close.

"Ms. Cyrus," a night nurse walked in. "I know this is not a good time, but we need to know what you plan to do with your daughter's remains. The hospital can only keep her for a day or two, before we're forced to deem her state property. At that time, she would have to be cremated."

Had it not been for Lexy blocking my way, I would've found the energy to leap from my bed and strangle the shit out her crude ass. Aware that she must deal with this type of misfortune everyday, and chalking it up to that being the reason she was taking my situation so lightly, still, there was a certain delicacy needed when handling the newly bereaved.

"Remains…remains…is that what you think of my child? Is that how you refer to her? Get out! Get the fuck out you heartless bitch!" Lexy had to hold me down, as my body began to take flight. I seriously wanted to fuck her ass up.

Frightened by my reaction to her question, the nurse jumped at the elevation in my voice, and dashed out of my room without haste. My heart was too heavy. *This could not be happening,* I thought. After all the emotions I had gone through to finally get to the point of accepting my pregnancy, and accepting the idea of being a mother, was now all in vain. This was too cruel.

Although Lexy understood my outburst, she knew better of me. She just looked at me, and shook her head. With a kiss to my forehead, she got up and went after the nurse to apologize on my behalf. Out in the hallway I heard, "Ma'am," as Lexy called after her. "I truly apologize for my girlfriend's behavior, but you must understand our position. Anyway, don't worry about Jada, which is our daughter's name, I'll take care of everything. She will receive a proper homecoming; at no expense to the government. Thank you." The nurse realized how insensitive she had seemed. She wiped the single tear that dangled from her cheek, and she too, apologized for her lack of compassion.

Minutes had passed before Lexy re-entered the room. She had taken a moment to gather herself. Her face was flushed from where she wept outside in the hallway of the hospital. Lexy returned to my bedside and asked, "How are you feeling Danielle?" She tried to remain strong.

"Lexy, I just keep asking myself why? Why me? Why her? She was innocent—pure. I would give anything to trade places with her. How could something so horrible happen to someone so perfect?" I sobbed loudly, "Oh God…it hurts so bad. What are we going do?"

Lexy couldn't do anything but hold me, as she rocked from side to side. I felt her tears, as they ran down her cheek onto my shoulders. I knew her pain.

Without a doubt she was really hurting, but she tried to remain steadfast for me. I was grateful to her for that, because someone had to hold us together.

Chapter Twenty-Four

"Ms. Cyrus," It was around 2:00 A.M. in the morning when I was awakened. I opened my eyes and Lexy was still asleep by my side. She looked so peaceful, poor thing had to be exhausted. I lightly stroked her head, as I was filled with so much love for her. "Ms. Cyrus," a masculine voice demanded this time. Struggling, I focused my vision. "I'm detective Richard, Miami homicide. I know this may not be a good time, but I need a statement from you, while the incident is still fresh in your mind."

I stared at him confused for a few seconds, before saying, "Homicide?"

"First off, please accept my condolences for your loss. Unfortunately, I don't know how you feel and I can't even imagine the pain you're in. But I do want you to know that I plan to do all I can to catch the animal that did this to you and your baby. Ms. Cyrus, can you think of anyone who may want to cause you or your baby harm?"

Anxiously, the detective awaited my reply; pen and paper in hand, ready to dictate my every word. Distracted by his title of homicide detective, I was about to say no, I didn't know anyone that would want to harm us. Until, that day with Malik suddenly ran across my mind. Malik did say one way or the other my pregnancy would be terminated. My eyes watered, as I reminisced on his exact words, then I spoke, "Yes, detective…actually the absent father of my child, Mr. Malik Michaels." And with those words spoken Lexy woke up.

I gave detective Richard all there was to know about Malik, all except his blood type. Addresses, phone numbers, friends, associates, you name it, I supplied it. "Why do you think Mr. Michael's would want to harm you and the baby?" The detective asked.

"When Malik first learned that I was pregnant, he was not happy about it at all. He said and did things that only a mad man would do. Adamantly, he gave me money for an abortion, but I didn't go through with it."

"Hmm," the detective mumbled, as he scribbled in his notebook.

"A few weeks ago," I continued, "I met Malik at a local coffee shop on Collins Ave. I wanted to be honest with him about not having the abortion; I felt he had a right to know whether, he wanted to be in Jada's life or not. After all, biologically he was still her father. His reaction towards my viable pregnancy was not surprising, but it did scare the hell out of me, and his words haunted me for a long time." Quoting him verbatim, *"one way or the other, this bastard child of yours will be terminated!"*

His words exiting my lips, sent chills down my spine. "Detective, honestly, I didn't think anything of it at first, because weeks had gone by free of any abnormalities. I should have taken heed to his threats, and maybe Jada would still be here with us today." Weeping, I turned to Lexy and mouthed the words...I'm so sorry.

All that had happened was my fault; I had led her to believe that Malik was harmless. Lexy's eyes were filled with tears that waited to fall. Unable to look at the hurt on her face anymore, I turned and faced the detective.

Rhetorically speaking he said, "So, he threatened you and you never told the authorities?" Quickly reviewing his notes, before closing the pad, "Ms. Cyrus, you should always take any and all threats very seriously. I'm sorry you had to learn the hard way, but if he is indeed responsible for what happened to you and Jada, rest assured that I won't sleep until he is rightfully punished. I'm going to let you rest for now. I think I have enough information to go question Mr. Michaels. I may need to contact you for more information, but I will try and let you rest from all of this first." Retrieving my hand, which lied lifeless at my side, "My family will be praying for you and your family." Gathering his belongings, detective Richard gave Lexy a nod, and was out the door.

Lexy sat in complete silence as she massaged her temples. "Danielle, you've been through enough, so I'm not going say what it is that I really want to say to you. But don't ever down play someone's threats or promises again. Do you understand what I'm saying?" Staring me dead in my face, I knew she was pissed. She did not cope well under extreme circumstances, this I knew, yet, here I was again, stressing her out.

"Yes, I understand Lexy and I'm sorry."

Without exchanging another word, she climbed into my bed and held me. "We're going to get through this together so don't worry too much." Sleep deprived, we both fell asleep only moments after settling down. It had been a long emotionally draining day.

Due to my unfortunate circumstance, in lieu of a room in the maternity ward, I was housed in a regular hospital room, far away from anything maternal. My initial take on the segregation was that of an insult, but now, incapable of withstanding the jovial sounds of laughter and love that accompanied the birth of a child, I was grateful to them for sparing me.

Chapter Twenty-Five

Never had I imagined that two days after the birth of my child that I would be leaving with nothing, but memorabilia given to me by the hospital. Inside the fuchsia colored box was a picture of Jada taken by the hospitals photographer, a lock of her hair, and her birth announcement. Somehow, as I clenched a hold of the box, I was to feel closer to her. The items given to me by the hospital offered me some comfort; forever reminding me that Jada was real. She was my angel. And now, thanks to the hospital staff, I could look upon her face anytime I needed or wanted to. Having something… anything, other than my scars and my memories, validated my eight and half months of pregnancy.

The car was silent as we drove home. Too much hurt…too much pain. There was nothing left to say. Lexy and I had already consoled one another; we had already cried together and prayed together. There was nothing left to do, except heal. Thankfully, Maxine had been to our house already. She cleared out everything that could possibly remind me of Jada; I wasn't trying to forget her, I just knew the repercussions of coming home to a baby ready home, with no baby.

My sweet Max, she hadn't been the same since the incident. Shutting herself in from the world, she took the demise of Jada a lot harder than I thought she would. She hadn't visited me in the hospital either, but I received dozens of flower arrangements from her daily. I understood her reasoning for not coming, and I wasn't mad by far. Knowing Max for as long as I've known her, I knew she didn't handle death well at all. Her outer layer was tough, because it had to be. Managing a salon in the ghetto, she had to appear hard, and tough, but I knew the real Maxine. And she was fragile. Jada was someone she had grown to love, and she looked forward to her arrival just as much as I did. So, to her, she lost a daughter as well, and needed time to grieve the only way she knew how…in solitude.

Lexy took my things to the room, and offered to fix dinner, but I declined. I wanted to be left alone, so I asked her for some time to myself. I wasn't trying to disregard her; she had also lost something the same way that I had. I just needed some time alone with my thoughts.

Complying with my request, I think she wanted some time alone too. Inside my room, I got down on my knees and prayed, *"Lord, I know you make no mistakes, so I won't ask you why again. I just pray for strength and courage to go on. I know Jada's in heaven with you, and that in itself brings me peace. Jada, my sweet baby girl, if you can hear mommy,"* crying, *"I will always love you, but God loves you more and that's why you're with him. Watch over us all, and help us to heal. I will never forget you. You will forever be my angel. I love you…Amen."*

That night, as I climbed into my bed, I felt light; as if a massive burden had been lifted from my shoulders. I couldn't really explain it, but I felt an inner peace after my talk with God and Jada. And although I still felt the hurt of losing her, for the first time since her birth (and death), I was actually able rest. Not just sleep, but rest—peacefully.

Jada was laid to rest a few days after I was discharged from the hospital. Lexy and I didn't see the point in waiting the traditional week, like most people did. Financially, we were capable of doing it sooner, so there was no need to drag out the inevitable. The actual burial was the most critical first step toward recovery; the sooner we did it, the sooner we could begin the process of healing.

Although my days of coping seemed long, and never-ending, with every day that passed, I prayed a little more, and cried a little less. Everyone had been over to offer his or her condolences, and to see if Lexy and I needed anything. Even Kevin stopped by, which was surprising. I thought he only made appearances at social events, but I appreciated the gesture. Seeing him outside his normal element made me smile; I needed that. Maxine had come by several times and called me every day. She too, was trying to be strong for me, and I loved her for that.

The funeral was small and intimate; just a few close friends. I didn't feel the need to invite every one we knew, because they weren't an immediate part of Jada's life—short lived or not. We were determined to keep it simple and we did. Max offered to deliver a brief eulogy on my behalf, because neither Lexy nor I could do it. Privately, she and I were allowed alone time with Jada at the end of the ceremony. That was where we said our final goodbyes to her, before she was taken to her final resting place; adjacent to mine.

Chapter Twenty-Six

Months had passed since Jada's death, and Lexy and I were doing much better than we had been doing earlier. Attempting to have some normality about myself, I returned to work; but anyone who knew me knew that I was different. Everyone at work had been forewarned about the death of Jada and was advised not to extend any condolences. At that point, I was fed up with condolences. Lexy had not fully returned to work yet out of fear of me having a relapse; despite the fact that I continuously told her that I was OK. She insisted on being around more, so I let her. Truthfully, besides a few crying spells every now and again, I was starting to feel like my old self.

Some time had gone by since the last time I spoke with the cops about that dreaded day in the parking garage of my doctor's office. They hadn't found any factual evidence of foul play against Malik, so the investigation had died down somewhat. But in celebration of me feeling better, Max and I had made plans to catch a movie and have dinner. I really wasn't in the mood to go out, but I knew Max would not take no for an answer.

We met up at the AMC Aventura for the 8 o'clock show. Max had picked out the movie since I wasn't current as to what was playing. "Hey baby girl," she said as we embraced each other. "How ya doing?"

"I'm good Max, but if you plan on asking me how I'm doing all night we will end this night real early." I had to lay down law because I was in no mood for sympathy. I wanted to chill with my girl, get a lil' tipsy, and then go home and lay with my boo.

"Damn, aren't we grouchy?" Max insinuated.

"No, I just want to stop you before you start that's all."

"We cool?" I asked

"Of course…always," she replied.

The movie started off a little slow, but eventually picked up. I was so not focused on what was going on in the film. My mind kept wondering off. I was thinking about all that had happened and wondered if Malik really had anything to do with it. I mean he did threaten me and the baby. Financially, he had the money to make something like that happen. He was smart enough to not get caught and grimy enough to go through with it. I was just so unsure. It had been five months, and the detectives had nothing. Part of me wanted to go and question him myself. The other part of me wanted to hurt him first, and ask questions later. Either way, I was left feeling empty. Completely oblivious as to what the movie was about, I was relieved once it ended.

Hungry, we headed to our favorite Bar and Bistro for some food and drinks. Max and I would hang out at the Bistro whenever the weight of the world was on our shoulders. And right about now the weight of the universe was on mine. We sat at a round table near the bar and ordered two tequila shots with lime. The atmosphere was really nice. The lights were dim and the music was soft. The candle in the middle of our table was the perfect setting to a romantic scene. Too bad I was here with my home girl.

It was cool to just be chilling with Max. It felt a lot like old times. I had to admit my mind was freed and the weight of the world started to lift off my shoulders, as we sat and reminisced on some good old times. But just as I was starting to let my guard down to allow the alcohol to take its course, my blood suddenly ran cold. I looked up from my glass and saw Malik gazing over at me from across the room with a sinister grin on his face.

Caught up in a trance of evil, Max's voice faded as I stared at Malik. I was incoherent as to what she was saying; my focus was locked in on him like a hit man to his target. "Dee... Dee...what's wrong?" Max yelled. I could hear her, but I couldn't snap out of it. Without effort, I arose from my seat and walked over in his direction. Although unsure as to what I was going do once I reached him, I rushed to him with urgency. In pursuit of my target, unknowingly, I knocked innocent bystander's shoulders in passing. My blood went from cool to boiling, as he sat there grinning and flirting with what I assumed was his new piece of ass. My palms were perspiring, my adrenaline was pumping a mile a minute, and my heart beat rapidly: like a small explosion waiting for detonation. Once I was within arms reach and before he could part his lips to say anything…Smack! My fist smashed into his face.

"Bitch!" he shouted, as he balled his fist as if to strike me back. Oh how I welcomed that. All I needed was a reason to loose my cool all over him. As a warning, I gave his bitch one good look to assure her that she could get it too; just in case she was feeling a little froggy and wanted to leap. But like a smart girl, she just stared at the ground like a child being scowled. Malik wanted to knock the shit out of me; I could smell it on him. It was written all over his face; but instead, he just rubbed his chin. It was his next set of words that pierced my soul like a dagger.

"Shouldn't you be at home resting? I mean after all you've been through you should still be in mourning; not out in a Bistro getting drunk. Shit…you should thank me. Look at you; that baby's better off dead than with you. You're not mother material."

"What did you say you heartless bastard?" I asked as tears weld up in the corners of my eyes, "what the fuck did you say?" I screamed!

Realizing he said too much, Malik attempted to walk away. He grabbed his lady friend by the arm, turned, and began to walk towards the exit. Before I knew it, I had leaped from where I stood, like some kind of a gladiator, and jumped on his back like a wild tameless animal. I couldn't remember much of what had happened from that point on.

****

"What happened? Why am I bleeding?" I asked Max. She was sitting by my side patting my head with a cold washcloth.

"Baby girl you don't remember any of what happened?" she asked me with puzzled look on her face.

"No…well…I remember us being at the Bistro laughing and having a good time…then I looked over and—and…Malik! His ass was across the room looking at me with a stupid ass grin on his face. I remember walking over to him and smacking the shit out of him…and…" As I recalled the words that exited his lips, my body began to quiver, my heart sped up, and tears filled my eyes.

"He said that he did me a favor," I mumbled to myself. "And I'm not cut out to be a mother. He did it Max. Malik is the reason I lost Jada!" I screamed. "What kind of a man-no…fuck that, what kind of an animal does something like that and lives with a clean conscious?" I asked rhetorically.

I asked Max to leave against her will. I needed to be alone. She was apprehensive, but respected my wishes as long as I promised to check in with her later. Before she left she asked, "Do you really think he's capable of such a malicious act?"

"Now I do," I responded. Heavy heartedly, Max left my condo. Luckily, Lexy was away at work; she didn't need to hear me say that. I had to think. I had no idea as to what my next move was going to be, but I knew I had to be smart about my approach. Malik was a smart and powerful man. He wasn't someone you couldn't just accuse of murder without probable cause. I needed facts, I needed evidence, and I needed them quick.

Chapter Twenty-Seven

I sat in my living room in complete darkness. The only light that flickered was from a single candle on my window mantle. Candles had always formed a serene atmosphere that was great for easing all pressures of the world. Whenever I was stressed, it aided with the clearing of my mind and the relaxation of my spirit.

The day of my attack replayed over and over again in my head. I could still smell the awful scent of his cologne and feel the roughness of his un-manicured hands against my flesh. As I sat, dissecting that day inside and out, it finally dawned on me. Malik wasn't my attacker, at least not physically. He wasn't man enough to do his own dirty work. And he wouldn't be caught dead with cheap cologne and un-manicured hands. That son of a bitch had to have hired someone to handle his lightweight. Fucking coward!

No, I was not about to let him get away with what he did to me. I didn't care how powerful of a man he thought he was. Even the dirtiest of dogs shall have his day and Malik's was right around the corner. I needed time to get all my ducks in a row. Everything had to be perfect, so that when I presented my case to a detective, all evidence would be based on facts and not assumptions.

I didn't know how I was going to explain all of this to Lexy. I knew she would be against me going after Malik, but some things were much too important to ignore. I needed time to play detective and Lexy and I had been through enough already, so making her an accomplice would do our relationship no good. This was something I had to do alone, and I knew the only way to accomplish that was by breaking up with her. The thought shattered my heart into a thousand pieces.

Breaking up with Lexy was not the option I wanted, but it was the only realistic option I had. She had been so good to me throughout the whole ordeal; it burdened me to have to end it. I wasn't 100% sure if I was making the right decision, but I was sure that I couldn't let Malik go free. To avoid a long drawn out scene, I told Lexy to meet me for dinner. What better place to end a relationship with someone than in a loud crowded public place? The drama was sure to be kept at a minimum.

Lexy was absolutely dumbfounded as she listened to me talk. She seemed numb to my words, as if she was expecting them. I felt horrible. I wanted to take her into my arms and tell her why I was doing what I was doing, but I knew if I did she would only get in my way. And I didn't want to be with her and purposely lie to her anymore. I hated keeping secrets, especially considering how I had kept Malik a secret from her for so long. I made my peace with her over dinner and assured her that one day she would understand why I had to end our relationship.

As I stood to leave, I kissed her softly and almost broke down myself, but I chose to walk away before I allowed that to happen. I knew I was weak for her, so once I got up to leave the restaurant, I refused to look back. Damn that was hard to do.

My heart was heavy and my soul ached, as I cried myself all the way to my hotel room. I knew one of us had to go, so I had arranged to stay at a nearby hotel until the storm known as my relationship passed over. The condo was mine, which meant ultimately Lexy would be the one moving out. I didn't want to rush her, so I reserved a room for a few weeks to allow her time to relocate.

By the time I made it to the check in counter of the hotel, Lexy had already called me several times. I had to turn my phone off to keep from answering it. She had left three messages. I chose not to listen to them and erased them instead. I hated myself. I just hoped that once this was all over she would allow me to explain, and hopefully her love for me would allow her to forgive me, yet again.

Tomorrow would start the beginning of a new chapter in my life. Once Malik was revealed for the monster he truly was, I believed my soul, along with Jada's, could completely rest. I knelt down before God inside my suite and asked for his blessing, as well as his forgiveness. I asked for the strength to maintain as I dug deep into the skeletons of Malik's closet. I didn't know what lied ahead for me, but I knew I would have to encounter him once more in the near future and mentally I needed to be prepared.

Chapter Twenty-Eight

Restless, I awakened anxious and unsettled. All night I contemplated on how I was going to seek justice. Although proper justice was the right way to go, I couldn't shake the desire of wanting to seek violent revenge for my own personal gratification. Why should his only punishment be a jail sentence? No, I wanted more than that. His freedom wasn't enough. There was always the possibility that his loss of freedom could be reversed within a few years. He needed to loose something more valuable and dear to his heart, something extremely irreplaceable.

Sipping on my coffee at the small dining room table inside my suite, my mind raced with ideas of what I could do to get back at Malik. Kidnap his kid for a bogus ransom that I didn't want perhaps, or tell his wife about our affair…Yeah, that would break her heart for sure, but his conniving ass would probably sweet talk his way back in her good favor. So that wouldn't work. Then it hit me…Angela. Everyone knew that Malik's family was his pride and joy. Eureka! That was it! My target would be Angela. Pondering on how I could use her against him was going to take quite a bit of brain storming. I had to think of something that would absolutely destroy him.

Malik was a man who lived by certain shallow standards, so being in the spot light and envied by others was his claim to fame. He had to live a picture perfect life, with his picture perfect family, but I would reveal how imperfect his picture really was.

What did Malik despise the most? What would upset his perfect balance if ever brought to the light? I thought back on our past conversations and arguments during our time together, and then it hit me-infidelity. I couldn't get him on infidelity, because that just wouldn't have the same effect, so somehow I had to get Angela to cheat on him, and then make sure she was caught. Oh, the embarrassment would kill him. But to add insult to injury, she needed to be seduced by a woman, and I'd make sure the word spread like wild fire throughout his place of business. This would prove to be challenging considering that I didn't know if Angela was the type to be had, but fuck that; "all" straight women have homosexual tendencies, whether they ever act on them or not. Shit I use to be one-case proven.

Strategy became my primary focus. What was going be my technique? First, I had to learn her whereabouts. Learn her likes and her dislikes. Thankfully I already knew what she looked like, thanks to Malik's careless ass. Can you believe he still carried a picture of his family in his wallet—portraying a picture perfect husband? *Ugh*…the thought of him disgusted me. Looking up his profile on his company's website was sure to list some important facts about his loving wife. Knowing Malik's schedule like the back of my hand, I knew when he was working and when he was not; at least during most of the week. Only he knew his after hours schedule.

Feeling bold, I decided to take a more risky approach. Since Angela's only occupation was being a homemaker, I knew solicitors were apart of her daily routine. All I had to do was pretend to be the average sales person who was trying to earn an honest income. Working in advertisement, I had already possessed a keen insight as to how to present and execute a good sales pitch.

I didn't have a lot of time to really do any research, so I chose a simple product—life insurance. Compared to the high profile campaigns I dealt with regularly at work, life insurance was going to be a walk in the park. After two weeks of preparation, I felt ready. The day had come and I was completely confident in myself. An automatic "out of office" reply message from Malik's email, confirmed that he was away on one of his infamous "business" trips for the next three days, so the timing was perfect.

My plan was to introduce myself to Angela as a competent sales woman; offering a lucrative life insurance policy at a competitive rate. I would elaborate on how the funds could be used to satisfy any financial obligations left behind by her loved ones, along with pay for the final burial arrangements. And to play on her vulnerability, I would fabricate my own tragic story as a formality. And if she took the bait like I knew she would, I'd use that moment of sincere condolences to my advantage.

Chapter Twenty-Nine

The next morning, I phoned in to my assistant and advised her that I wouldn't be in due to a family emergency. Then I got dressed for my sales job, as I rehearsed my presentation in my head. Inside a brief case, I packed some pamphlets that I had downloaded off of an insurance website. It was amazing the stuff you could retrieve and alter from the Internet. They appeared 100% authentic. I had pricing guidelines, a toll free number to reach "customer service," and to top it all off, I even dressed the part: Hair up in a bun, two-piece skirt suit, natural sheer colored stockings, brief case with pen and paper, even a fake nametag that I got offline. I meant business.

On the drive over to Angela's, I kept thinking back on all my close encounters with her, making sure she had never really seen me. So far, there were no recollections of us ever meeting purposely, or otherwise. But we have had quite a few close calls. Once, Malik and I were eating at a beautiful expensive restaurant in celebration of our six months anniversary, and unbeknownst to us, the location of that restaurant was right in the neighborhood of where Angela's book club met twice a month. Of course, we had to have the ocean view, so it was located right on the main strip of South Beach.

Recognizing her from the photo in his cheating ass wallet, I had to be quick. Not wanting to alarm him that I knew the identity of his wife, I simply gestured to him to follow me to the ladies room. All I had to do was rub his dick with the ball of my feet. He knew this as my signature move whenever we were dining and I got horny. Just in the nick of time we had walked away from our table and were out of sight as Angela passed by. She was engulfed in casual conversation with her book group and I was in the bathroom getting fucked.

Their house sat at the top of a small man-made hill way out in North Lauderdale. It was a big beautiful house, only a few rooms shy of a mansion. Inside, I could see Angela through the open, uncovered windows. She was in the kitchen. It looked as if she was ending a phone call. Approaching the door, I grew a little nervous. Then I thought about my purpose for being there, and instantly, all inhibitions were lost. I rung the doorbell and waited for her to answer it.

She was more beautiful than I imagined. Her long sleek body frame was wrapped in a white silk house robe, revealing her hardened nipples as the morning air hit them. She obviously wasn't wearing a bra. Long honey blood hair hung low past her bust line. She was the exact brand of woman I thought Malik would be with. She was too beautiful to have any flaws, and too light skinned to be of a black ethnicity.

"Hello, how may I help you?" Her voice as sweet as any nurturing mothers would be. "Yes, hello my name is Kelly. I have been door to door in your neighbor hood for most of the morning and you are my last stop. I am here to speak with you about an affordable and much needed life insurance plan. It protects from the first day of enrollment and builds cash value over the years. I would only need about ten minutes of your time today ma'am. May I please come in?" Hesitant, but in agreement, "OK, ten minutes, that's all I have to spare."

Huge vaulted ceilings, floor sized windows, and a fireplace? Who needed a fireplace in South Florida was beyond me, but if you got the money why not. I followed her into the massive family room and took a seat as instructed. "I'm listening," she said as she crossed one leg over the other. Regaining my focus, I began my presentation. She seemed a little bored with the whole thing, so I amped it up a notch. Something real had to happen in order for her to bite. It was time to let out the fabricated story of how I lost my parents to a freak accident, and how I couldn't afford to bury them.

Tears flooded my face, as I told the story of how I lost both my parents to a four car pile-up one stormy day, and how I almost lost the house, which I raised in, due to unpaid bills and no financial substance. Empathetic towards my unfortunate loss, she became more attentive as I continued sobbing.

"I'm so sorry. I apologize for my outburst. I don't know why I told you, a complete stranger this story. I guess feeling the warmth of your home reminded me of how warm my parent's home use to feel." I lied.

"It's OK Kelly. I'm sorry to hear about their passing. Was it recent?" she asked.

"Yes, it was actually one year ago today. I guess the anniversary of it all is rooted deeper in my subconscious than I thought."

Handing me a handkerchief, "Oh, I'm so sorry sweetheart. I can't imagine what that must feel like. You shouldn't be working so hard today. Today should be used in observance of your parents."

"I know, but I thought by working it would keep my mind off of my own problems."

Half way smiling she said, "I hate to tell you this, but you're selling life insurance. Ironic don't you think?"

A sense of humor, I never pegged her for having a funny bone in her body.

"Look we are pretty much squared away on life insurance Kelly, so I won't be purchasing anymore; however, you look like you could use a friend. Why don't we have some lunch if you have the time, and we can talk about other things on a much happier note?"

Hook, line, and sinker—she took the bait. "I would like that very much; thank you." I accepted her lunch invite.

Angela turned out to be really cool. She had great conversation and was more interesting than I thought. Under other circumstances I would've liked to have known her for purposes other than revenge. For hours, we laughed and swapped stories in her living room as we ate the delicious meal she had prepared for us. At the conclusion of lunch, she insisted I took her number in case I ever needed to talk again. Somehow I felt that our conversation was more therapeutic for her than me. She admitted that it had been a long time since she had had basic girl talk. So before I left, I promised to call her soon so that we could hang out again.

Chapter Thirty

After weeks of living in a one bedroom hotel suite, I was relieved when I finally checked out. Lexy had already begun the process of moving per the text that I had received from her a few days ago. I tried not to let her moving out bother me, but I was only kidding myself. I was bothered and I knew I would miss her dearly, but there was a bigger picture at hand, and I had to remain focused.

Parked along the curbside of my condo, was a midsized moving truck. As I walked passed, I watched three men carefully place familiar objects onto the back of their truck. My front door was left wide opened, as I stepped inside my almost vacant condo. I hadn't realized how much of my stuff had been packed away in storage for the benefit of Lexy. Knowing the answer to my own question, I asked the men what was their purpose for being in my home?

"Alexis hired us to move her belongings. She was here, but she left about half an hour ago. She said you wouldn't mind us finishing up."

"No, it's OK. I figured that's who you were here on behalf of. Did she leave me a message?"

"No ma'am, I'm sorry she didn't."

I wasn't surprised. I didn't deserve a message. She had finally let me go. It had only been three weeks since we broke up, but I thought for sure she would have asked me to help her move. I was wrong. Instead, she had hired movers to avoid unnecessary contact with me. I didn't blame her.

Strangely, as I watched strangers carry out her belongs the pain of it all was still present, and it didn't hurt any less. It had been made official. She and I were through. But I remained optimistic, and hoped that once all my bullshit had been resolved, that she'd forgive me and we could pick up the broken pieces of our relationship.

"So did I tell you about this Jamaican woman I met last week at the club?"

"No Max, you didn't. What about her?" I strained to hear her over the loud noise throughout the sports bar.

"Nothing, except she's hot. I mean the girl's head is fire. It really surprised me that she was of Jamaican descent. Most Jamaicans I know claim to hate gay people."

"You'd be surprised how many gay people are Jamaican Maxine. Granted, most of them are probably closeted gays, but gay none the less."

"Yeah, you're right. Her family doesn't even know about her. They have their suspicions, but won't face them."

"Max, people tend to fear what they don't understand. That's probably why her family doesn't want to believe the obvious."

I tried to stay attentive to during my conversation with Max, but I kept thinking about Angela and how comfortable I had become with her. Being around her made me smile and she had the sweetest most feminine laugh I had ever heard. We had been meeting up for lunch for the past few weeks and talked over the phone almost every day. It was safe to say we had developed a close friendship. To say I was smitten with her would be an understatement. I didn't know what it was about her, but I was no longer sure about my plan for revenge. I still wanted Malik's head on a platter, but I didn't want to hurt Angela in the process. *Damn! What had I done?* I wasn't supposed to fall for her, but she had gotten to me in the worst way.

Chapter Thirty-One

Angela and I had planned to go out for dinner. Malik was away once again on one of his infamous business trips and she didn't want to spend the weekend alone. I didn't mind being in her company, so I was elated when she asked to spend some time with me. Angela was a classy lady. Malik's attraction to her was obvious. She was well groomed from head to toe, not a single hair ever out of place. Standing at 5'7" without heels, her makeup always remained fresh and flawless. I longed to touch her intimately.

Inside the car, on the way to the restaurant, I kept looking over at her thighs. Her skirt was just the right length to toy with my imagination. I knew a woman of her caliber had to be clean-shaven with pretty pink lips. I hoped that I'd soon get to kiss them. My pussy thumped hard against the seat of my pants, as I thought of Angela and all the things I wanted to do to her.

Inside the restaurant, I ordered two Long Island Ice Teas because I really needed a stiff drink. I wasn't sure how Angela would act inebriated being that we never drunk together; therefore, I asked the bar tender to lightly lace her drinks with alcohol. Me on the other hand, I needed mine strong, so I asked for double shots in all my glasses.

The live jazz band took my breath away as I listened in admiration, while sipping on my drinks. I knew falling in love with Angela was very possible and quickly approaching. I was no longer set on her being my revenge; instead, I wanted to whew for my own personal gain. She looked stunning and moved gracefully, as we drank and chair danced to the beats of Miles Davis, Anita Baker and Kenny G.

Hopeless, I knew I could fall in love with her without even trying. Had I fallen in love with her? I asked myself. At this point I didn't care if I had. Although I still cared for Lexy, I knew that chapter of my life was over. I had put her through too much in the past and she deserved more than what I had given her.

Generously intoxicated, Angela grew more talkative. Together we had consumed six Long Island Ice Teas. She became more free with her tongue and opened up to me in ways I never imagined. She shared very intimate secrets with me that I'm sure Malik still doesn't know about. Her stories were dated as far back as to when she was a child and she and her "female" cousin would make out at night when they were supposed to be asleep. That alone shed some inkling of hope for me. As I watched her transform from classy conservative to relaxed and flirty, I felt that that was the perfect opportunity for me to dig a little deeper.

Moving in closer to her, I stared firmly into her eyes, "Angela let me ask you a personal question. Are you a happy with your life; the overall quality of your life?" Being very careful about her response, she finally answered, "Most times I feel like I am, but other times I feel somewhat incomplete." Saddened by her response, she excused herself to the restroom. I assumed she needed a break from our conversation, before she completely broke down. I almost felt bad about what I asked her but thought better of it. I was new in her life. Whatever caused her to feel incomplete had nothing to do with me.

Moments later, Angela re-appeared to the table with slightly swollen and reddened eyes. It was obvious she had been crying.

"Are you OK?" I asked her.

"Um, yeah I'm fine," she lied checking her mascara in her hand mirror.

I knew she wasn't OK, but I didn't want to pry, so I suggested that we ended the night. No words were exchanged as we left the restaurant, which made for an awkward ride home. Angela sat staring out of the window as if she was in deep thought. Although I wondered what was on her mind, I didn't dare ask. Then, just as I was about to say something to lighten the mood she spoke.

"Kelly I'm not ready to go home just yet. Can we go somewhere quiet so I can clear my head?"

Empathetically, I replied, "Sure, anything you want. I know the perfect place."

A quick detour led us in the direction of the beautiful South Florida beaches, to my own personal place of serenity.

Warm and humid, the ocean breeze trespassed into the crack of my car window.

"Do you want to go for a walk?" I asked her.

"No, I just want to sit here if you don't mind."

"No, sweetie I don't mind…whatever you need."

"Wow, do you know how long it's been since someone's taken into consideration my needs over theirs, or the last time I was made to feel important?" she said.

"Angela you are important and you deserve the best every day," I assured her.

Apparently she was naive when it came to knowing her worth. My palms started to sweat and my heart raced as I attempted to tell Angela how I felt about her. I braced myself as I opened my mouth to speak. But before the first words could come out, she had placed her right hand to my cheek, turned me to face her, and then gently kissed my lips! I melted on contact. I wasn't sure why she kissed me, but I indulged in it for the moment. Those few seconds of kissing her felt like years of internal peace; I did not want it to end. Not now-not ever.

Am I her rebound? Was she kissing me and thinking of her husband? Was she too drunk to realize what she was doing? There were so many unanswered questions…so many uncertainties. Then a single teardrop fell from her eyes and broke our connection; I pulled away to look at her.

Confused, I asked her what was wrong? She grew hysterical then pulled the door handle and jumped out of the car. Running frantically to the shoreline, Angela fell to her knees. Cautiously, I followed behind her until I reached where she stopped. In silence, I took a seat next to her and looked out at the ocean.

Dried up tears had settled atop of Angela's flushed cheeks, as she sat tightly wrapped in a light blanket that I had given her from the trunk of my car. I was tempted to hold her as she stared off in the distance of the moon, but I refrained. I knew that this was not the time for that. I had learned a long time ago that sometimes the best medicine for someone in her state was a silent shoulder to lean on. Therefore, I did nothing and waited silently for her to speak.

"Kelly I need to tell you something, but I'm not sure how to say it."

"Please, just say it Angela." I was shitting bricks. I didn't know what she was about to say.

Still focused on the moon she asked, "Why do you think I excused myself at the restaurant?"

"Um, I don't know, but it's OK. We really don't need to talk about it."

"No, we do need to talk about it, because you were the reason I had to excuse myself from the table earlier."

"Me...?" I said surprisingly. "What did I do?"

"It's not what you did. It's what you're doing." Confused I waited for an explanation.

"Kelly, I'm falling in love with you," she said as she got up and walked closer to the water. In disbelief of what I'd heard, I leaped up from where I sat and ran after her.

"What did you just say to me Angela?" I asked seeking confirmation of her statement.

"You heard me…I think I'm falling in love with you."

Elated, I gently grabbed her by the arm and turned her to face me. "OK, now I need you to look me in the eye and repeat those exact words one more time."

Without blinking she looked me in my eyes and repeated, "I think I'm falling in love with you…and I know the feeling is mutual."

Unable to deny her allegations, I happily confessed my feelings for her, and relieved my burdened shoulders that late evening on South Beach.

Chapter Thirty-Two

Day broke, and the sun never looked more beautiful than it did that morning. I awoke with Angela is my arms. Angelic as only she could look so early in the morning, she looked over at me and suggested it was time she got home before Malik called. Malik…a person I had forgotten about since my attraction to his wife.

Disappointed, I said, "OK." I mean what was I gonna do—hold her hostage? Although parts of me still sought revenge on Malik, the other part that had fallen in love with Angela insisted that I left him to answer to God. I wasn't sure what I was going to do. The only thing I was sure about was that I loved Angela and optimistically hoped for a future with her.

Knowing how Angela felt about me made it that much harder to say good-bye once we reached her house. Returning her to a man who didn't deserve her irritated me. I wanted to rescue her from all of his infidelities and show her the life she was meant to have. I knew she loved me; it was in her eyes. I wanted to feel her lips again, so I moved in closer to kiss her good-bye and was startled by the sound of her house phone ringing. We both jumped.

"That's him," she said nervously. He won't stop calling until I answer."

"What are we going to do Angela?" I asked, needing something to leave with.

"I don't know." She said turning to walk in the house. "I'll have to call you later. I need some time to think."

And that was the end of that. She stepped inside and closed the door behind her, and I was left standing on her door step with so many mixed emotions.

Twice…Malik had taken someone I had loved away from me; I was furious. If only I could prove he had something to do with my assault, I could rid him of both mine and Angela's life for good. But would she still want and love me unconditionally? I didn't know the answer to that question, but it was a risk I had to take.

Thankfully, I had remained cordial with a few of Malik's colleagues from his job. I always kept those I befriended within a close proximity, because you never knew who you would need later in life. On my drive back home, I wrecked my brain recalling all the people he had introduced me to, and out of those, the one's I kept in my personal rolodex. I had to be wise when choosing my accomplice, because if my plot leaked, Malik's reaction could be detrimental to all those involved.

Then a name came to mind just as I pulled into my driveway—Jesse. I knew Jesse would not hesitate to assist me. He was soft on me from the first moment we met. The only reason he had behaved himself was because Malik was a powerful businessman. He too, did not want to burn his bridges and that was perfectly understandable and strongly recommended.

Once inside, I pulled out my phone catalog and found Jesse's well-tucked away business card. He had given it to me a while back, told me to hold on to it in case things didn't work out between me and Malik. At present, I was glad that I had held on to it. Briefly, I contemplated on what I was going to say, and then I picked up my cordless phone and dialed Jesse's number. I didn't want to alarm him by telling him the truth right away, so I began our conversation with irrelevant small talk.

"Hey Jesse, it's me Danielle; Malik's friend. How are you?"

"Hey Danielle, how are you? Last I heard you were no longer Malik's friend."

"Yeah that's old news. Anyway, how are things with you?"

"Everything's fine, but to what do I owe the honor of your call?"

"I really hate to involve you, but I need to speak with Malik about an important matter. And since he won't answer my calls, I thought that I could reach him on his private corporate number. Do you happen to know the number?"

"Danielle, I would really like to help you, but Malik keeps that number extremely confidential. Only the top dogs have it. I could give him a message if you would like."

"No, that wouldn't do much good. Jesse, I'm going to level with you. Malik did some real foul shit to me...illegal shit, and it's up to me to prove it."

"Uh huh, I'm listening," he said.

Knowing that I had his full attention, I began telling Jesse everything I needed to tell him without telling him too much. I made sure to lay it on real thick, that way he would have no choice but to help me. However, I did avoid telling him about the pregnancy. I felt that that was too much information and none of his damn business.

Jesse listened attentively as I continued to bad mouth Malik. Although most of what I told him was lies, the truth remained the same. That son of a bitch had hurt me and I was not about to let him get away with it. Filled with empathy for what he thought Malik had done to me, he agreed to meet me at his office, which also happened to be Malik's office.

We agreed to meet at nine o'clock that evening. He knew the night guardsmen and would be able to get me access into Malik's office. Knowing he was risking his career by helping me, I promised him complete immunity once Malik was revealed for the snake he really was.

It was about fifteen minutes until the hour when I arrived outside of Malik's office building. Jesse was leaving the parking deck as I pulled up. I had memorized his phone number so that I could call him once I arrived.

"Hi Jesse, I'm here."

"Great! Come on in."

He assured me that the night guardsman had been forewarned of my arrival. Lucky for me, their company switched security guards more than prostitutes turned tricks. I was a little apprehensive because the last guard that worked for them had seen me with Malik a few times. But Jesse had assured me that this was a new employee, and that he had only been working for them for the past two months.

As I walked through the luminous 10-story glass building, I noticed a bald husky white male seated at a half round cherry wood desk. Barely looking up from his newspaper, he directed me to Jesse's office. Usually, I would have snapped at his lack of common courtesy, but in this case I was glad that he didn't get a good look at me in case he needed to identify me later.

On the fourth floor Jesse waited for me by the elevator. He was tall, dark, and handsome. Attributes I never noticed before. Back then, looking at another guy was totally out of the question and vice versa. No one ever attempted to cross that line with Malik. Either his associates had the upmost respect for him, or they all feared him. I couldn't tell the difference.

"Hey Danielle," Jesse said with a sweet innocent kiss to the side of my cheek.

"Hey Jesse," I replied.

"Still as beautiful as always," he flirted.

I didn't want to be rude; therefore, I simply smiled and said thank you. After a few wasted minutes of being nice, I turned the topic of conversation back to Malik. Realizing that I was there for a purpose, he apologized for taking up so much of my time then directed me down the hall where Malik's office was located.

"Thanks Jesse, I know exactly where it is. I won't be long. Where are you going to be when I'm done?" I asked. Emphasizing the fact that his presence was not welcomed beyond that point.

"I will be waiting right here outside of my office," he said. Unsure of what I was looking for he said, "Danielle I'm not 100% comfortable with us being here and I really don't want to know what you're truly looking for, but if you need me I'm here for you."

"Thanks Jesse. I know where you are if I need you." Then I left him in the hallway and entered Malik's office.

Nothing much had changed. His coffee mug still sat near the right side of his computer—half empty, his favorite football team jersey hung from the wall behind his office door, and ironically, he had a family photo on his desk. I cringed, as I recalled the countless times we'd had sex behind those cream colored walls, and how he fucked me so passionately, while his wife's photo stared back at him. Who did he think he was? The more I thought about what he had done to me and what he continued to do to Angela, the more I hated him.

Picking up the photo of Angela off of his mahogany rectangular desk, my core softened. I knew she would never forgive me if she knew what I was up to. I loved her, and I didn't want to hurt her or her daughter; but some things were unforgivable. As I thought about my own loss, tears filled my eyes and I quickly dismissed whatever remorse I had started to feel for his family.

"Life isn't fair little girl. Not in my world and soon not yours," I said, as I put the photo back on his desk.

Ruffling through the papers on Malik's desk, I came up empty. I opened filing cabinets and desk drawers, but still nothing. Damn, I wanted to scream. I had only one shot of finding some dirt on Malik and so far, I hadn't done a good job at it. But I refused to leave without having something on him.

I sat down in one of the vacant chairs in front of his desk and thought hard about Malik's habits for a moment. Then it hit me. He kept a safe behind the jersey on his wall. I knew he used the safe to hide incriminating evidence about his infidelity, because he would always stick receipts from our rendezvous in there when he thought I wasn't looking.

Hotel receipts, credit card statements, mortgage payments, plane tickets, cell phone statements, money…etc. Oh yeah, Malik was a great provider. My bills stayed paid on his dime. I knew if there was anything to be found out it would be in that safe. I wondered if he was smart enough to change the code. It used to be our anniversary date.

I walked up to the jersey and carefully removed it from the wall. I tried the code I knew, and to my surprise it had been changed. But with men being only half as smart as women, I knew to try the anniversary date of his marriage. A date he didn't think I knew. *09-23-02-Click…* The safe opened. That sick bastard actually had the audacity to use the date from which he took vows—promising utter fidelity, as the code to unlock his alternate lifestyle. Wow!

And just as expected, he had records of everything. I assumed he saved everything for tax purposes, because what person in their right mind would keep such detrimental evidence. I scrambled through all the receipts, all the lies. Malik turned out to be a bigger hoer than I thought. There were thousands of dollars worth of receipts there, and all were current. There were so many different women…so many different names. That son of a bitch itemized his lovers by putting their names on their receipts. Poor Angela, she wasn't even second or third on his list. He had *soooo* many women. It made me sick to my stomach to learn of all his lies. Hell, based on the dates on some of those receipts, he had even cheated on me.

There was one bank receipt in particular that stood out to me. It was a withdrawal receipt from Malik's bank with my name on it for five thousand dollars. The date on the slip was right around the time I was attacked. Stapled to the receipt was a man's name and phone number—B.J., 555-241-3232. My heart skipped a beat as I stared at the name of my alleged attacker. Quickly, I folded the papers and put them in my pocket. I made sure to put everything back the way I had found it and exited Malik's office. As promised, Jesse was waiting outside of his office.

"You find what you needed baby girl?" he asked.

"No…actually I didn't find anything," I lied. I didn't want Jesse involved anymore than he already was. The less he knew the better.

We walked in silence toward the elevator. Very appreciative of his help, I thanked Jesse for meeting me on such short notice, and kissed him softly on his cheek as I got onto the elevator. As the doors were closing I heard him say, "You should've been mine." Then the doors shut and seconds later I was back in the lobby.

The guardsman was not at his station when I returned to the lobby. I assumed he was away conducting a security check of the premises. Thankful for his absence, I left the building, got into my car, and drove back home. I didn't know what my next move would be, but at least I had a beginning. I could go to the cops, I thought. But what good would that do without "hard-core" evidence? Police officer's usually didn't arrest people without probable cause, and a name and phone number was not reason enough to arrest someone.

Satisfied with my efforts for that day, I poured myself a glass of wine, stretched out on my leather sectional, and listened to some smooth jazz on the radio. I didn't' want to ruin whatever small chance I had of catching Malik; therefore, I settled on hiring a professional to finish what I had already started. I had a pretty good lead, and all they had to do was follow up on it. A bit fatigued, I topped off my glass of wine and headed towards my bedroom. That's where I spent the remainder of the night.

Chapter Thirty-Three

The next few months were strenuous. Keeping what I was doing a secret from Max and Angela had become a full time job, but I managed to do it. I had hired a private detective to pick apart Malik's life piece-by-piece. Every move he made was being watched and recorded. There was nothing personal about his life anymore. I had the most elite in the detective business, and for the money he was being paid, nothing was left unexamined.

It had taken three long months to finally break the case, but I will never forget that day when my P.I. called me.

"Ms. Cyrus," a deep defined voice asked.

"Yes, this is she," I responded.

"We got him! I managed to get a hold of some old phone records, and there was a voice message from Mr. Michaels to the man hired to attack you."

"What?" I gasped.

"Yes, we got him! I need to speak with you in person to give you all the details."

I agreed to meet the detective at a local bar in my neighborhood so we could discuss our next move. I was frantic on the inside. Emotionally, I was all messed up. Parts of me were happy that we had caught his ass red handed, but the other parts of me were nervous about having to face him and prove that he had conspired against me. Nervous, I threw my hair in a ponytail, grabbed my coat, and was out the door.

Seated at the end of the bar was Raymond, my private investigator. He wasted no time indulging himself. He had already ordered a drink and was sipping slowly. I took a seat next to him as he began to pull out surveillance photos, copies of written phone messages from Malik's assistant, bank statements...etc. He explained everything to me in great detail without holding back anything. I sat baffled by his findings.

Then in mid sentence, he stopped talking for a quick second to check my status before he continued, "Danielle, are you OK?" Amazed by what I was seeing and hearing, I responded, "Yes...please keep going."

"Ok, now the next thing I reveal to you will be a picture of Malik's accomplice. Are you sure you can handle seeing the face of your attacker?" Seconds had passed before I responded, "as ready as I'm going to be Raymond."

Quickly, I redirected my eyes to the floor, unsure if I was actually ready to see his face. But through the corner of my eyes, I could make out what Raymond was doing. Two photos were being placed on the bar in front of me, an 8x10 and a 5x7. "Here is your attacker. His name is Benjamin James." Slowly, I lifted my eyes from the floor and with great hesitation set my gaze on the photos in front of me.

He was not the man I had imagined in my head. I expected a burly, balled man, with a big gut, and a hairy face. But what I got was just the opposite. He didn't look like someone who would do what he had done to me. He was a handsome man, and resembled someone well respected with a wife and kids. A lot like Malik. Literally, I gawked at the man in the photos.

"Raymond, do you know anything about this man?" I asked.

"Yes, he's an ex-cop turned bad. He got fired from his squad some years ago. He was accused, and convicted of domestic violence against his now ex-wife. He lost his badge, his wife, his life, and his mind. Despite his present day chosen profession, he is still highly respected, highly paid, and highly recommended; especially, when someone in Malik's tax bracket needs a…for lack of a better words—a cleanup man."

*A clean up man…*the shit had become too surreal. I felt like I was watching some old gangster movie or something. I desperately needed a drink. I waived my hand for the bartender's attention and ordered a shot of tequila straight—no chaser.

Raymond and I spent the next two hours discussing the next step in our pursuit of justice. He suggested that we had enough solid evidence to go to the cops and file murder and attempted murder charges against Benjamin and Malik. Raymond insisted that I had a strong case, and with the right lawyer, there was no way either of them would walk away free.

All the recorded conversations between Malik and Benjamin, along with the messages retrieved from Benjamin's answering machine, were in safe keeping at Raymond's office. I thanked Raymond for all his hard work and settled my tab with him. In return, he gave me all the evidence he had on him and wished me good luck.

On the drive to the police station I thought about Angela. I wondered what she was doing at that exact moment and if she would still want to be with me once I'm found out. With Lexy out of my life, I really needed Angela to remain by my side. Her love for me would be tested now, more than ever. I hoped for the better, but prepared myself for the worst.

Miami's Police Department was one of the largest in Florida. Cop cars were aligned all around the building and in every car that arrived to the precinct was a newly awaiting convict. I couldn't wait for the day when Malik's ass was in the back of one of those cars.

I parked my car and went inside the station. People were scattered everywhere. Phones rung off the hook and criminals were on either side of me; no matter which direction I faced.

"May I help you ma'am?" an officer seated behind a desk asked.

"Yes, my name is Danielle Cyrus, and I am here to press charges against my former boyfriend, Malik Michaels." I said confidently.

"And for what exactly Ms. Cyrus?" she asked looking really confused.

"Murder," I replied, as I handed her all the evidence I had.

She carefully examined all the evidence I had given her and nervously stumbled to her feet.

"Ms. Cyrus, please take a seat. I'll go and get one of our homicide detectives to assist you."

Chapter Thirty-Four

The days were long and the nights were endless, as I awaited the outcome of the police's investigation. In the meanwhile, I had taken a break from Angela. I knew things had to have been hectic in her home with the investigation and interrogation of her and her husband's life. I wanted to talk to her and explain my actions, but I was too afraid. So I waited to see if she'd reach out to me first.

Angela, apparently pissed with my disposition with her, called me demanding we talk. I wasn't sure what she wanted to talk about, but the inflection in her tone warned me that it was serious. I was left to assume that she wanted to talk about the charges I had pressed against her husband. We agreed to meet at the pier that overlooked Ft. Lauderdale Beach.

Gazing out at the still waters of the sea, I rehearsed what I was going to say to Angela. My normal place of serenity suddenly didn't seem so serene. My spirit was too unsettled, and didn't allow me to be seduced by the calmness of the ocean, as it once did. Footsteps audible in the distance, I knew it had to be Angela. I didn't want to turn to greet her. I didn't want to stare into those innocent eyes that made my knees buckle. I didn't want to face my fate, but I had to.

Angela stood before me; even more beautiful than when I saw her last. She was wearing a yellow and blue sundress that swayed with the pattern of the wind. Her hair was pinned up in a bun, and she wore a pair of yellow beach sandals that complimented her dress; she was stylishly flawless. Seeing her again gave me butterflies in the pit of my stomach.

"Walk with me," she instructed, and I followed without haste. For the first few minutes of our walk we remained quiet. I knew she was trying to gather her thoughts before speaking. Then she said, "I know who you are Danielle." *Huh...* I gasped. I didn't try to deny it. There was nothing I could've said, so I waited for her to continue. She stopped walking and turned to me.

"Danielle, I knew who you were the moment you showed up on my door step. You and Malik weren't as careful as you thought you were, and I wasn't as naive as you conceived me to be. At first, I only meant to entertain your ridiculous approach, but when you started to cry over the death of your parent's, well, that caught me off guard. Therefore, I couldn't call you out on your bullshit at that moment. Honestly, I thought you needed a friend, and quite frankly, so did I. I had planned to tell you on so many occasions, but it never seemed to be a good time. Then, I fell in love with you, and couldn't bring myself to tell you out of fear of losing you. Funny I know. Here is the woman that's been sleeping with my husband for however long and I'm worried about losing her in my life."

She picked up her pace again only to stop suddenly. "Why did you really come to my house that day?" she asked. Taken aback by her question, I felt there was no need to lie anymore, so I confessed to it all. My heart broke as I told her the truth about my affair with Malik and my plan of revenge. Drenched in my own soiled tears, and down on bended knees in the middle of the beach, I begged Angela for her forgiveness.

Surprisingly, she wasn't at all moved by what I had said to her. She had dealt with the realization of her husband's infidelity long before meeting me on the beach; therefore, she was no longer affected by it. Her heart had grown numb. Reaching down to help me up from the ground, she calmly said, "Danielle, I forgave you the moment I fell in love with you."

Chapter Thirty-Five

Six months later, and thousands of dollars in lawyer's fees, Malik was finally served with a warrant for his arrest. I won't ever forget that day. I woke up that morning with the feeling that something good was going to happen. It was a Thursday, and I was in very good spirits. I did everything as I normally would; took a shower, combed my hair, drank my coffee…etc. And just as I was leaving for work my phone rang.

"Ms. Cyrus?" A monotone voice inquired.

"Yes," I replied.

"This is Miami Dade Homicide Department, with a courtesy call alerting you that Mr. Malik Michaels has been arrested. He is being held on first degree murder charges."

My heart nearly jumped out of chest as I screamed, "Yesssssssssss!"

Over the next couple of weeks while Malik's lawyer's conjured up evidence in his defense, my attorney, along with homicide detectives, coached me on what to expect at the trial. They wanted to make sure I was emotionally and mentally prepared to face off with him. I wasn't sure if I was ready, but I had come too far to turn back. As they coached me, in return, I coached Angela. She had been staying with me since our meeting on the beach. Unbeknownst to me, she had filed for a divorce and was separated from Malik when she met up with me. She was convinced that their life together was over and she had finally found happiness with me.

Malik's lawyer's had been in contact with Angela as well; she was to be a witness in his defense. The idea of that didn't sit well with me, but she did have a daughter to consider, and I didn't want to get in the middle of their relationship; at least no more than I already had. But I knew Malik didn't stand a chance of getting away with what he had done, so I wasn't that concerned about her testimony. Besides, she was on my side, and wouldn't say anything derogatory against me.

Surprisingly, Angela had taken living with another woman quite well. I thought she would've had a relapse, but she had no interest in her old lifestyle anymore. Jasmine, her daughter, decided to stay with Malik; she hadn't accepted her mother's status in my life. Maxine, she was partial towards my involvement with Angela as well. She refused to get close to her and openly conveyed how she didn't trust her motives. Max couldn't get past the fact that Angela knew about my affair with Malik yet, she still wanted to be with me. I appreciated her concern, but I trusted Angela, and that was all that mattered.

The first day of court was nerve wrecking. Angela and I walked into the courtroom hand in hand. Malik arrogantly sat beside his lawyer. As usual, he had that same stupid ass smirk on his face he always had when he felt untouchable. One look at him, and I was immediately enraged. I couldn't wait to hear what the snake had to say in his defense.

"All rise," the bailiff announced as the judge took his rightful place on the bench. Both my lawyer and Malik's, were allowed to present their opening statements to the judge and the jurors, before calling their witnesses to the stand. I was the first to testify.

"I call Ms. Danielle Cyrus to the stand." My lawyer said.

"Ms. Cyrus, do you swear to tell the truth, the whole truth, and nothing but the truth, so help you God?" the bailiff swore me in.

"Yes," I replied, with my right hand raised.

On the stand I stared blankly into Malik's face. I held nothing back as I told the court everything he had ever said to me, along with our numerous volatile occurrences. I told them about the day in my condo with Ariel, how he threatened her and put a hole in my wall. I spoke on the fact that he knew I was pregnant and how violently he reacted. Then finally, about the meeting we had at the coffee shop just weeks before my attack. To conclude, I quoted verbatim his comments from that night at the Bistro. The jury gasped at my allegations, and at the thought of such a model citizen being capable of such malice.

By the time I was done, there wasn't a dry eye in the courtroom; besides, that of Malik's. Even Angela shed a few tears. I wasn't sure if she was crying out of shame of Malik's infidelity, or if she was crying for me. Either way, she was in pain; unfortunately, I had no remorse for her at the time.

"Thank you for your testimony Ms. Cyrus. I am truly sorry for your loss. You may step down." My attorney gestured.

Raymond, my private detective, took the stand after me. I listened as he testified on my behalf. His testimony was critical to my case, because he was the one who provided all the evidence that led to Malik's arrest. The jury seemed pleased with the information obtained from Raymond, and all the evidence provided was legally submissible on my behalf.

Throughout the trial I managed to hold my composure, but shit hit the fan for me when Malik was asked to take the stand. My chest tightened and my heart raced as he walked across the room. Emotionally, I had endured way too much. I thought they were going to have to carry me out on a gurney. As he opened his mouth to speak, my blood rushed through my veins, causing my pulse to beat erratically. My skin grew clammy and sweat beads fell from my forehead. My attorney noticed the change in my demeanor and asked the judge for a short recess so that I could recuperate.

Angela followed me to the restroom to make sure I was OK. I told her I was fine, but I wanted to be alone. She understood my position and excused herself from the ladies room. I knew she was worried. She thought I was upset with her, but I wasn't. I didn't blame her for her testimony. She did what she had to do for the sack of their child.

She was asked to comment on the character of her husband, and she told what she knew to be true of him. In her life, in the world they shared, he wasn't a violent man. He was the perfect husband, the perfect father, and a great provider. She knew of his extracurricular activities, but for the sake of Jasmine, she kept that tucked away. No, I wasn't upset with her. I just hated him and needed some fresh air.

Bending down at the sink, I threw water on my face. I needed to gather myself before I lost it in the courtroom. The hatred I felt towards Malik was inhumane. I wanted Malik to *die* in prison. I wanted his death to be slow, and agonizing. He needed to suffer to the point where death would be a reward in lieu of his pain. Knock...knock.

"Danielle, are you OK?" Chuck, my attorney, asked.

"Yes, I'm fine. I'll be out in a minute." I shouted from behind closed doors.

I took one final look in the mirror before I went back into the courtroom.

Malik was still on the stand, as I entered the room. Without hesitation, court was back in session. Malik's lawyer interrogated him in his defense, of course. He made him look like a saint, and in return, Malik humbled himself on the witness stand. I wanted to throw up as I sat there and listened to all the lies he told the court. Chuck had to restrain me during his testimony. He didn't want me to be held in contempt of court. Tears streamed down my face, as he denied all allegations. *"Heartless bastard,"* I mumbled to myself.

"Thank you for your testimony Mr. Michaels. You may take your seat," his lawyer dismissed him. I couldn't believe that Negro had the audacity to mouth the words "I love you" to Angela as he past us. The expression on her face materialized her dislike for him. In an attempt to console me, she placed her right hand on my shoulder. Malik took heed to her gesture and sent a sadistic glare my way.

At the end of all witnesses' testimonies, our attorneys delivered their closing arguments, and court was adjourned to allow the jury time to deliberate. We were to meet back the following morning for judgment. My nerves were too raveled to sleep that night. Sex would have been a perfect nerve stabilizer, but Angela and I, hadn't gotten to that point in our relationship yet. She was still not ready to go all the way and I didn't want to rush her.

The next morning, the courtroom was even more packed than the day before. Malik was dressed sharp and still had that stupid ass smirk on his face. The jury stood to deliberate, and I had an eerie feeling in the pit of my stomach as the deliberation began.

"In the case of Danielle Cyrus versus Malik Michaels, we, the jury, find Mr. Malik Michaels, innocent on charges of first degree murder and attempted murder. In the charge of accessory to murder, we, the jury, find Mr. Malik Michaels, guilty."

"What!" I yelled out loud.

"Quiet, Ms. Cyrus!" the judge demanded.

"How long can he get with accessory to murder charges?" I asked Chuck through muffled whispers.

"With his bank account and reputation, he probably would only get 3 years maximum with parole after one. Damn it!" Chuck growled.

"Mr. Michaels, we will re-gather here in one week for sentencing. You are out on bail until that time. Court is adjourned for one week." The judge announced.

With the bang of his gavel, he dismissed the courtroom, and that was when I snapped. All I remembered was reaching for my boot, a loud bang, people screaming, and Malik's dead body hitting the floor.

Chapter Thirty-Six

(South Florida Penitentiary)

"So Ms. Cyrus, everyone wants to know, as well as myself, where did you get the gun?" The young eager news reporter asked.

Smiling, dressed in my prison orange jumpsuit, I walked towards the barricaded windows, and glanced outside, "Let's just say, Malik wasn't the only one who had connections with highly paid respectable people."

"I see…" the reporter said, as she made notations in her notebook. "Now, the story line headed that Mr. Benjamin James had a gas leak, and was torched to death in his own home while awaiting his trial; did you have anything to do with that?"

Still smiling, I looked outside at the birds flying free; something that I would never be again…free. Then I reiterated, "Like I said before, Malik wasn't the only one who knew highly paid respected people."

Disappointed with my response, she realized that she wasn't going to get anymore information out of me other than what I had already given her, so she packed up her camera crew and got the hell out of dodge.

Back in my cell, I thought back on recent events. Prison wasn't quite the outcome I had imagined. I just couldn't live with knowing Malik may have been free in a year. So during a moment of insanity, I traded my life for his. I had no real regrets only that I hurt the three women I loved most: Maxine, Lexy, and Angela. When Malik took Jada away from me, I too, died in that hospital with her. That incident left only a shell of a woman behind; but justice had finally been served. *An eye for an eye Malik; an eye for an eye—you bastard! May you never rest in peace!*